RAFAEL'S CONVENIENT PROPOSAL

RAFAEL'S CONVENIENT PROPOSAL

BY

REBECCA WINTERS

First published in Great Britain 2004
Large Print edition 2004
Harlequin Mills & Boon Limited,
Eton House, 18-24 Paradise Road,
Richmond, Surrey TW9 1SR

© Rebecca Winters 2004

ISBN 0 263 18088 3

Set in Times Roman 16½ on 18 pt.
16-0704-44235

Printed and bound in Great Britain
by Antony Rowe Ltd, Chippenham, Wiltshire

CHAPTER ONE

"FOR those of you just joining the Jack Hendley Friday Night Live show broadcasting from New York, we have the gorgeous Ms. Mallory Ellis in studio with us this evening."

The band played a little theme music and the audience clapped.

"If you have eyes in your head, you could be forgiven for thinking she's a world-class supermodel or top box office movie star, but you'd be dead wrong. At twenty-nine years of age, Ms. Ellis has the distinction of being one of the youngest female executives ever featured in *Financial Wizards of Wall Street.*

"A top honors graduate in corporate law from Yale University, Ms. Ellis was snapped up by Windemere Cosmetics, a struggling Los Angeles based firm. In three short years under her guidance, the company not only has a new name, 'Lady Windemere Cosmetics,' it has also gone global. So far the profits keep rising

5

which is good news for the employees who now own stock in the company.

"According to the magazine article, her undisputed genius lies in profit and loss savvy, but tonight we're hoping she'll reveal some of the secrets of her phenomenal success story."

From far away, the audience couldn't tell the TV host's eyes glittered as he studied her. "According to a source close to you, you're a woman who knows what women want, and you put women with the right credentials in charge. Did you always plan to be a big female tycoon?"

There was an edge to his question rather than a teasing tone. She'd seen him in action before. Jack Hendley was a male chauvinist who had fixed ideas about a woman's place in life. That was all right with Mallory. A lot of insecure men had the same problem.

Coming on this show was the last thing she'd wanted to do. But when Liz Graffman, the seventy-year-old widow who owned Lady Windemere Cosmetics, received a call from the television network asking that its vice president fly to New York and be on the Jack

Hendley show, Mallory couldn't say no to Liz's plea.

Lady Windemere Cosmetics would get the kind of exposure on his show you couldn't buy at any price.

Over the last thirty-six months, Mallory's relationship with Liz had become like that of a favorite great-aunt and niece. Surely Mallory could stand a half hour of being patronized by one of television's long-standing night talk show hosts.

"A tycoon by definition implies someone who owns a company or many companies. I only work for one," she corrected him with a friendly smile. He didn't smile back which was no surprise since he could sense she was refusing to play ball with him.

"However to answer your question, when I was old enough to think about the world, there was only one thing that drove me; my insatiable love for surfing."

His eyes flared because he hadn't been expecting that response. "Where did you grow up?"

"Huntington Beach, California."

"That explains it. Were you a good surfer?"

"I won a few western regional champion-ships at Redondo Beach and Malibu."

Several wolf whistles resounded along with the clapping from the listening audience.

"At this juncture I'm sure every eligible male watching would like to know if there's a future *Lord Windemere* waiting in the wings somewhere."

The man was so predictable she had to stifle a moan before she said, "No."

"Does that mean—"

"It just means no," she broke in on him with a purposely engaging smile that lit up her brilliant blue eyes. Mallory had done her share of dating. She loved men as much as the next woman, but she didn't confuse her personal and professional life by getting too close to any one man. In fact she couldn't see it hap-pening in the foreseeable future. Maybe one day.

"So what happened to turn you from a surfer into a corporate attorney?"

She'd made him uncomfortable with her brief, unrevealing answers. Good. It was about time he'd asked her a question relevant to her being on the show in the first place.

"If I wasn't surfing, I was reading beneath a beach umbrella. At an early age I became addicted to comic books. My father has a huge collection dating from the forties to the present which he treasures to this day. I must have read every one of them and particularly liked the stories about the Amazon women from Paradise Island with their secret powers."

He turned to the audience. "Put her in one of those sexy little outfits, and she'd look just like them." His remark provoked more whistles and cheers.

Mallory ignored the remark. When the din died down she said, "During the WWII years, the man who created that series once said that if women were given a little more time and the added strength they'd develop out of the war, they'd begin to control things in a serious way. When women ruled, there wouldn't be any more war because the girls wouldn't want to waste time killing men."

Another loud burst of applause broke out.

"Needless to say, those comments found a resonant chord in me. From that moment on I decided I would be one of those women who would begin to control things in a serious way."

By now most of the women were on their feet clapping while the band played some more theme music. When it finally subsided and they sat down again the host said, "So it's true that since you've taken over the reins, Lady Windemere has become an all women-run company?"

Mallory nodded, then cocked her head. The unconscious gesture caused her long, glistening hair, the color of dark mink, to slide over one shoulder.

"That's right. Women want to be beautiful for men, but they dress and put on makeup to pass a woman's inspection. You're married, Mr. Hendley. When your wife asks you if you like her in pink or red lipstick, what do you say?"

"That I like her no matter what she wears."

"Exactly. You sound like a good husband who knows how to stay out of hot water. But

you're no help because you don't want to of-
fend her by giving her a wrong answer.

"The female managers and employees at
Lady Windemere don't have to be careful in
the same way. They'll tell a customer the truth
and create a pallet of colors just for her to
make her feel her most beautiful and confident.
In the end she'll buy more products and stay
loyal to the brand for life."

"In other words, I won't be able to find a
man to wait on me if I walk into one of your
stores."

Her remarks had gotten under his skin. She
sat back in the chair resting her hands on the
armrests.

"No."

"Some might argue that you're sexist."

Mallory had been waiting for that salvo. She
re-crossed her long elegant legs. "After taking
a good look at Windemere, I saw what I
thought needed doing in order to turn it into a
promising business concern.

"If I were in the hierarchy of a company
that didn't cater exclusively to women, natu-

rally the question of whether to employ males or females wouldn't be a relevant issue.''

His brows lifted. ''You mean you wouldn't fire all the men and put a bunch of women in charge, say—if you headed a national auto parts chain that was going under?''

The man refused to let the subject go. Maybe that was why his ratings were slipping. Mallory was beginning to understand why the network was planning to install a woman co-host. They needed a feminine element to offset *his* sexist outlook on life.

''If it were in my power to hire and fire, I'd see who was productive and who wasn't. Whether male or female, they'd be gone if they didn't have the company's best interest at heart.''

He sat back in his chair, eyeing her speculatively. ''We only have a minute left before we have to go. I see a lot of hands in the audience.'' He turned to them. ''What's your question?''

''How about a date after the show?'' a half a dozen guys shouted.

Mallory had known better than to expect any questions about Lady Windemere cosmetics, not after the way the host had handled the program.

''Thank you, but my busy schedule won't permit it,'' she answered with another smile. ''You've been such a great audience, I want you to have some samples of Lady Windemere products I brought with me. They'll be outside the doors when you leave.''

While the audience cheered and clapped, she pulled a gift-wrapped package from her purse.

''This is for your wife, Mr. Hendley. Compliments of Lady Windemere.'' Actually it was from Liz who'd placed a personal note inside.

''I'm sure she'll enjoy your products. Thank you.'' He put it to one side. ''Before we sign off, can you tell the audience what your plans are after you leave New York?''

''Yes. I'm on my way to Europe to visit our newest store in Lisbon.''

"So it's business as usual. Did you pick up a degree in Portuguese while you were at Yale too?"

His condescension bored her.

"Don't I wish. Fortunately for me the new manager communicates in excellent English and Spanish as well as her native tongue."

He turned to the band and started speaking Spanish to one of the Hispanic members, supposedly to impress his audience, but Mallory's thoughts were on the new manager she was going to visit, Lianor D'Afonso.

The Portuguese woman exemplified the company's top female executives abroad who were intelligent, sophisticated, lovely, feminine and possessed great business sense.

During the three week training session in Los Angeles where six European managers had come together, Mallory had felt a particular fondness for the single, twenty-nine-year-old Lianor.

When they weren't working, Mallory had taken her to many of the tourist sites. They'd discovered that they had a lot in common and agreed on many things.

Mallory had grown up an only child, but if she could have had a sister, she would have wanted someone as delightful as Lianor.

It had been almost four months since the training session had ended. Mallory had to admit she was looking forward to seeing Lianor who'd be meeting her plane tomorrow evening.

"We're out of time folks," Jack Hendley said, switching back to English to regain Mallory's attention. "It's been a real treat to have you on the show, Ms. Ellis."

Naturally he didn't ask her to come back again. She hadn't been any fun.

"Thank you for inviting me, Mr. Hendley." She shook hands with him and stood up.

As she left the stage to a round of applause and more wolf whistles, she could hear his mind saying, "Why don't you go on home and find yourself a man. It'll make a real woman out of you, honey."

Mallory had heard it all many times before.

Relieved the show was over and she could get back to normal, she left the studio. A cab came along to take her to her hotel. She'd been working nonstop for a long time and was looking forward to a change of pace the short trip to Portugal would provide.

Rafael D'Afonso grimaced when he realized the new Lady Windemere cosmetics boutique on the rua Da Plata appeared to be thriving.

It was June. By now he'd hoped the American-based company where his sister had been installed as manager would have been forced to close its doors. She would have had no option but to look for another job. Maybe then he could have talked her into giving up her Lisbon apartment and coming back home.

Unfortunately his hopes on that score were dashed last week by an offhand comment she'd made about the first quarter's earnings being even higher than the home company had projected.

She loved her new job and wasn't about to give it up.

Since their parents' death twelve years ago, he'd been watching out for his strong-willed sister who'd already turned down several marriage proposals. If she immersed herself in business much longer, she would miss out on the most important role of her life—becoming a wife.

Lianor was already twenty-nine, six years younger than he was. Time was running out for her. One day soon she would mourn the fact that she had no husband, no children. He refused to let the scars from her past ruin the rest of her life.

Though Rafael was weighted down by bad news that hadn't fully sunk in yet, he decided now was the perfect time to use it as leverage to force her to come home and embrace the life she was meant to live. All he wanted was her happiness.

As he entered the boutique located in Lisbon's Chiado district, their gazes met. She was still helping a customer. Her other two employees were both busy as well. Taking a deep breath to curb his impatience, he headed for her private office. He would wait for her no matter how long it took.

To his relief she joined him within a couple of minutes. He put his cell phone away and hugged her. After she'd sat down behind her desk she smiled, looking supremely pleased with herself.

"Take a chair, brother dear. You're prowling like a hungry wolf. What's put that grave look on your face?"

He remained standing. "There's no easy way to say this. As you know, Maria has experienced unbearable stomach pain lately. She finally went to the doctor and was diagnosed with cancer. She's in the very last stages. He said she won't be leaving the hospital."

"Oh no—" Lianor cried. In the next instant she'd leaped from the chair and had thrown her arms around him again, dissolved in tears. "The poor thing. What about Apolonia? Does she know yet?"

"No." He'd left his ten-year-old daughter playing with a friend. His housekeeper, Ines, was watching them. "It's going to come as a tremendous shock."

"I can't believe it. Maria's too young. I thought she'd be with you until Apolonia was all grown up."

"So did I," he muttered.

"This is awful," she lamented.

It was. Since his wife, Isabell, had died of pneumonia within weeks of giving birth, sixty-two-year-old Maria who'd been a maid in Isabell's parents' home, had taken on the role of surrogate grandmother to Apolonia.

Lately his daughter had grown quiet and seemed moody which was not her normal nature. No doubt her worry over Maria, who hadn't been able to hide her discomfort from the family for several months now, was at the root of her uncharacteristic behavior.

He feared that when Apolonia heard that the only mother-type figure she'd ever known was on the verge of death, his daughter wouldn't be able to handle it without Lianor being there to take her place.

"That's why I came here instead of phoning you. I want you to come home with me and we'll tell her together tonight."

She pulled out of his arms, wiping her eyes. "I'm sorry, Rafael, but I'm afraid I can't."

He blinked in shock. "Why? What's more important?"

"The vice president of the company is flying in from New York. I have to pick her up at the airport in two hours."

"You mean the notorious Lady Windemere?"

His sister looked wounded. "I'm sorry that her being a brilliant woman lauded by Wall Street makes you see her in such an unfavorable light, Rafael."

"How else can a man view a woman who's hard as nails, as the Americans say."

"You're wrong about her, you know. She's *not* the owner, and she's *not* Lady Windemere. For your information it's the name she gave the company to revitalize and romanticize it. The rising profits are the proof of her business acumen.

"Her name is Mallory Ellis. And I'm asking you not to speak about her in such a derogatory way again."

He couldn't help it.

Mallory. Even her name sounded too masculine to his ear. There was nothing soft about Lianor's new idol. The idea of his sister spending any more time with some hard-boiled female powerhouse who eschewed marriage and family was anathema to him.

''How long is she going to be here?'' his voice grated.

''Tonight through tomorrow night. She'll fly home the following day.''

Rafael swore under his breath.

She put a placating hand on his arm. ''Look—don't say anything to Apolonia for a couple of more days. I promise I'll come home as soon as Mallory has flown back to the States.''

He fought to tamp down his frustration. ''It doesn't look like I have any choice. Where's this American paragon going to stay while she's here?''

''At my apartment.''

''No, Lianor, you can't do that.''

''She has become a friend, Rafael. While I was in California she went out of her way to show me one of the most wonderful times of my life. We stayed overnight at her parents' house and they were nothing but gracious to me.''

Rafael had no idea all that had gone on while she'd been out of the country.

"I'm certainly not going to let her go to some sterile hotel room. Besides, you always wine and dine your friends and business associates at home."

"I happen to live at our family's pousada which makes it convenient to entertain guests."

His sister eyed him frankly. "Taking her home would have been my first choice, but knowing how you feel about my job, I thought it best to stay away."

"It's your home too," he averred forcefully. After a pause, "Bring her there tonight." He decided he wanted to meet this dangerous stranger who'd become friendly with his sister so quickly. "I'll arrange for a room."

"This is very important to me, Rafael. Will you give her the Alfama suite?"

The Alfama? His first inclination was to remind her that he reserved the best suite in the palacio for heads of state and royalty. But he caught himself in time.

"I'm prepared to do that favor for you... provided you do one for me later."

"Of course."

He eyed his sister through veiled eyes. She had no idea what she'd just agreed to. "I'll inform Vaz she'll be staying there for two nights."

"Thank you," she whispered before kissing his cheek. "I love you. I know you're worried sick about Apolonia's reaction. Over the next few days I'll try and think of someone who could take Maria's place."

"I already have the perfect person in mind," he murmured, "but we'll talk about it when I can have your undivided attention."

After giving her another hug, he left her office in a better mood than when he'd arrived. Apolonia and Lianor adored each other. His sister wouldn't be able to turn him down when he asked her to take over Maria's role.

It would bring Lianor back into their world of mutual friends and men. To make certain she said yes, he would visit Maria in the hospital here in Lisbon right now and tell her

Lianor had agreed to be there full-time for Apolonia. That would calm Maria's fears.

As for Lianor, when she went to see Maria, the older woman would thank her for doing her duty as Apolonia's loving aunt, that is if she could still communicate. Lianor wouldn't have the heart to argue with a dying woman.

His sister didn't know it yet, but she needed his daughter as much as Apolonia needed her.

Driving into the city from the airport, Mallory thought she'd never seen anything as romantic as Lisbon against a twilight sky. Draped over seven hills with the Tagus river flowing through, the sight enchanted her. She said as much to Lianor who'd picked her up outside the terminal in a silver Jaguar.

The other woman nodded. ''If you think this is beautiful, wait till you see my family's home overlooking the Atlantic. That's where you'll be staying while you're here. It's just a half hour from Lisbon on the Estoril coast with its own private beach.''

''It sounds heavenly.''

"Do you want to stop for something to eat first?"

"Thank you for offering, but they served a meal on the plane before we landed. I'm still full."

"If you're sure."

"Positive. Right now I just want to absorb everything."

"That's how I felt when I flew to Los Angeles for the training session. After it was over and you took me to the airport, I couldn't resist spending a few days in San Francisco. The plane landed at about this same time of night. For a moment I thought I'd returned to Lisbon because the two cities reminded me of each other."

"Me too," Mallory murmured, "but Lisbon is ancient. That's what makes it so fascinating. Judging by the success of your first quarter earnings, putting the shop in the medieval part of the city was the right decision."

"I *know* it was. We're always busy, and getting busier."

"That'll be music to Liz's ears. She and I discussed the store's location with the marketing and sales departments at length. I'm glad the company decided to take the risk, and I'm particularly glad they hired you.''

''I'm the one who's thrilled.''

Mallory found herself warming more and more to Lianor. In fact the whole Windemere staff had taken to her. Several of them had even commented that from a distance, she and Mallory looked like they could be sisters with their tall, curvaceous figures and long dark hair.

But upon closer inspection, Lianor's olive skin and dramatic brown eyes were in direct contrast to Mallory who'd inherited a peaches-and-cream complexion from her mother. Still, the observation had pleased both of them.

''Loving your work is a blessing, Lianor. Not everyone does. Without the right manager that store wouldn't be doing as well, and certainly not this soon. Liz has arranged for you to receive a bonus in your next paycheck for all your hard work.''

Lianor beamed before whispering her thanks. ''When my brother first heard I'd been hired to manage a cosmetic shop on the rua Da

Plata, he warned me I'd be out of a job in a few months because it would fold in the old district. Instead the locals and tourists flock to it.''

Mallory's eyes danced. ''From what you've told me, your brother is one of the most successful businessmen in the country. But because he's a man, he doesn't understand that a woman will stop whatever she's doing long enough to try out new cosmetics.''

Her friend nodded. ''Rafael's wife, Isabell, the one I told you about who died ten years ago, was a natural beauty. She rarely used makeup or lipstick around him because he didn't like it. He says all men prefer women au naturel, so he discounts its importance.''

''But he can't discount the earnings of your shop now, can he.''

Again her friend grinned. ''No, and it's killing him to admit it.''

''In that case, it might be interesting for him to see the results of our marketing department's studies done among men throughout Europe. I brought a chart with me. The Portuguese statistics, particularly, would be very illuminating if he ever took the time to look at them.''

''Tell me!'' Lianor cried like a co-conspirator.

Mallory brushed the hair away from her cheek, getting caught up in the excitement with her. ''Only twenty-one percent of Portuguese men prefer their women without lipstick.''

''I knew it!'' her companion blurted.

''The other seventy-nine percent is divided; twenty-eight percent love their women in shocking pink lipstick, followed by seventeen percent who love lip gloss. Sixteen percent like pale pink and the softer shades. Ten percent prefer red, and seven percent like beige or brown.''

Laughter broke out on Lianor's lips. ''Rafael's forte is marketing. As he says, 'It's all in the figures.'''

''He's right. They don't lie.''

''I can't wait to show him that chart, but I'm afraid it will only upset him more.''

''Why? Surely he wants you to succeed!''

''It isn't that. He's been unhappy ever since I was hired.''

This was the first Mallory had heard of it. "I don't understand. After college you worked in the marketing division of a large department store several years before joining the company."

"That's true, but I wasn't the manager."

"With your talents and background, you should have been," Mallory stated emphatically. "What is it about your being in charge that bothers him so much?"

"That's not the problem. Simply put, he wants me to get married, settle down and raise a family. You'd have to be a younger sister *and* Portuguese to understand. It's a male thing here. He's my older brother and protective and—"

"Say no more," Mallory broke in. "I've met his type before. They're alive and well in America too. You would know what I meant if you could have watched the television talk show I was on last night." She proceeded to tell Lianor about her experience with Jack Hendley.

Lianor nodded. "Sounds like Rafael. He's afraid I'll never meet a man as long as I'm running a store, let alone one that sells women's products. What he doesn't realize is, I could go out every night of the week, and still not come across a man who truly interests me.''

''My sentiments exactly.'' Mallory flashed her a compassionate glance. ''In order to placate your brother, you might remind him that part of our new advertising campaign is geared to reaching the male population—that group looking for a special personal gift for his wife, girlfriend, or mother.

''Knowing what the Portuguese men want, the company is prepared to cater to their individual tastes. Assure him you'll be meeting a lot of male customers as time goes by.''

''Unfortunately Rafael wants that miracle to happen *now*. Tonight!''

They both broke into laughter.

''It sounds like he loves you a lot,'' Mallory observed.

''He does, and it's mutual.''

Mallory already knew that. No matter the topic of conversation, since she'd first met

Lianor, her brother's name always managed to creep into the conversation.

Lianor flicked her another glance. "Your father was so nice and laid-back. Does he ever get upset because you're not married yet?"

"Maybe," Mallory murmured honestly, "but neither he nor mom has ever said anything. It's probably because they didn't marry until their early thirties. They don't want to come off sounding like hypocrites."

"My mother was just nineteen when she married my father. Rafael proposed to Isabell when she was only twenty."

Rafael again. "What do you think's the reason he hasn't remarried?"

Her companion let out a deep sigh. "It isn't for a lack of women! Most of the time I'm appalled at the lengths they go to in order to capture my brother's attention. But the plain truth is, he loved Isabell so much, it almost killed him when she died. Since then he's been devoted to Apolonia, and has buried himself in work."

Apolonia. The niece with the beautiful name.

"Maybe you need to get busy and find him someone *he* could love. You know him better than anyone else. If he married again, he might not be quite as concerned about your single status."

"Don't count on it," Lianor muttered. "However you've given me an idea to solve a problem that's been plaguing me since he came to the store earlier today with bad news. It has shaken me for several reasons."

The unexpected emotional throb in Lianor's voice alerted Mallory that whatever was on her mind was serious. "Do you want to talk about it?" she ventured quietly.

"I shouldn't have brought it up, but you're too good a listener."

"I feel the same way about you. Why do you think I came to Portugal?"

Lianor's head jerked around for a moment. "What do you mean?"

"You're running the store so well, I didn't really need to come. But since I was already in New York, it seemed the perfect opportunity to take you up on your offer to visit."

"I'm glad you did, Mallory."

''So am I.''

''Tomorrow's Sunday and the shop will be closed. I'll take you sight-seeing. Give yourself a couple of weeks here and we'll be able to cover the whole city on foot if you want.''

''Oh I want,'' she assured the other woman. ''If only I *could* take two weeks off to do nothing but soak up the atmosphere. Nevertheless tomorrow I'm hoping to sleep in and then lie on the beach. I haven't had a real holiday since I went to work for Liz.''

''That's too long to go without,'' Lianor chastised her, in the nicest possible way of course.

Mallory's mouth turned up at the corners. ''Now that we have that settled, tell me about your brother's bad news.''

In a few minutes she'd put Mallory in the picture.

''Maria's virtually irreplaceable,'' Lianor confided further. ''We all love her, and Rafael has depended on her so totally, I'm worried. Of course he has Ines, his housekeeper. He can rely on her to help him with my niece, but it's only a temporary solution.

"I have to face the fact that word of Maria's fatal illness changed his whole world today. As for Apolonia, the loss will be devastating when she finds out Maria isn't coming back."

Mallory could only agree.

"My closest girlfriend from childhood has recently come out of an ugly divorce from her Spanish husband. She's back from Madrid and needs something to absorb her time right now. Rafael has always known Joana and liked her. So has Apolonia. I'm thinking if she came to help, it would be good for all three of them."

"You could be right," Mallory said. "Given time, they might even fall in love. How nice would *that* be. Your best friend becoming your sister-in-law."

"Don't think I didn't used to fantasize about it. However that was a long time ago, before Rafael fell for Isabell and dashed both our dreams."

"You mean yours and Joana's."

"Yes. She was crazy about my brother."

Somehow that news didn't surprise Mallory, not if he was as remarkable as Lianor—in all the ways that really counted.

At this point they'd reached the coast, a breathtaking sight this time of night. The smell of the ocean intoxicated her. Waves crashed against the sand, creating froth that stood out in the darkness. She could hear the pounding surf, that familiar sound she craved almost as much as she craved air to breathe. She didn't know how much she'd missed it until now.

They rounded a curve on the winding highway. Suddenly she let out a cry. There was a baroque palace on a cliff in the distance, lit up as if it hung in the sky. ''I can't believe what I'm seeing is real,'' she whispered. ''What's the name of it, Lianor?''

''Rafael and I call it home, but the tourists know it as the Palacio D'Afonso.''

Speechless, Mallory's head turned, unable to do anything but stare at her friend.

''It was one of several small palaces built by King Pedro the Second of Portugal. Some historians claim he had it built and named it in honor of his brother King Afonso who was paralyzed and died at the age of eleven. Others say he built it out of guilt after deposing

Afonso and exiling him to the Azores while Pedro was acting regent.''

''Ooh—that doesn't sound good.''

Lianor chuckled. ''By the time my great-grandfather inherited it, the cost of keeping it up forced the family to turn it into a hotel so it wouldn't pass from the D'Afonso line. Historians still argue whether it began through one of Pedro's illicit liaisons with a courtesan. We'll never know for sure.

''After our parents died at sea, Rafael was the one who made it into the prosperous resort it is today. Because of his genius, our family now owns half a dozen small castles and palaces in various parts of the country which have been converted into tourist resorts we call pousadas.''

To the average onlooker, the D'Afonso family would seem to be living a fairy-tale existence. But like all human beings, they had their own share of private tragedies to deal with.

''Did you ever ask your brother if you could manage one of them?'' Mallory couldn't help asking.

"No. I've always wanted to do my own thing."

"We're kindred spirits, Lianor."

"I know. That's what's got Rafael worried."

"Now you're making me nervous."

"Please don't be. I'll have you know he has made arrangements for you to stay in the best suite. Just last week it was occupied by the President of Mexico and his wife."

Mallory shook her head. "I don't want or need special treatment."

"Maybe not, but you're going to get it. I know how hard you've worked since law school. It's time for you to be pampered, so sit back and enjoy it."

A chuckle escaped Mallory's throat. "When you put it like that..."

"Thank you for not arguing with me. We'll be there in a few minutes."

CHAPTER TWO

"INES?"

Rafael walked in the family's private entrance at the north end of the palacio. He headed for the kitchen, grim-faced.

"I'm here. How is Maria tonight?" she called back to him as he pushed open the double doors.

"She's deteriorating fast."

Ines' eyes watered. "Apolonia is missing her already."

"Where is she?"

"She and Violente went into the other part of the palacio to look for some postcards while they waited for Violente's father to pick her up in reception. I told Apolonia she had to be back in a half hour."

He took a steadying breath. "Now that school is out, I don't like the idea of adding to your burdens by asking you to take full-time care of her." Ines was in her early seventies

38

and slowing down. "Which one of the maids do you trust to watch her for a few hours each day to help you out?"

"Either Nina or Brianca."

Rafael rubbed his jaw and felt the rasp. "Isn't Brianca a little young?"

"She's eighteen, but she's very responsible and she likes Apolonia. It would be good for your daughter to have someone who will play with her."

Ines was right about that.

"Will you talk to Brianca then?"

"First thing in the morning."

"Good. Tell her I'll make it worth her while financially until Lianor is prepared to take over."

"She has agreed?" his housekeeper cried out with joy, putting her palms together beneath her chin.

"Not in so many words yet, but she will," he vowed with such ferocity, Ines blinked. "Don't say anything about Maria or Lianor yet. I don't want her to know what's happening until I'm forced to tell her Maria won't be coming home again."

"Claro," the older woman said before turning away, sniffing.

He checked his watch. Lianor ought to be arriving with her guest anytime now. "I need to make some phone calls, then I'll go find Apolonia. Thanks for all your help, Ines. *Boa noite.*"

"Boa noite, Rafael."

The Palacio D'Afonso proved to be a masterpiece of baroque and Moorish architecture mixed together. Mallory heard Lianor call to her, but she was too busy drinking in everything to talk.

Checkered marble paved the floor and ornate staircase of the enormous entrance hall. She lifted her head to take in the beauty of its lofty dome exquisitely painted with flowers and birds. Between the rich decorative art and paintings on the walls, she stood there spellbound.

"Wander around to your heart's content," Lianor said. "Your suitcase has been taken upstairs. Give me a minute to make certain your room is ready. I'll be right back."

"This palace is so magnificent, I'm speechless," Mallory murmured. "You don't have to hurry on my account," she added with a smile. "I might just stay here indefinitely."

"Wait till you see where you're going to sleep tonight." Lianor left her with that provocative thought before she started up the staircase where several elegantly dressed hotel guests were just descending.

The couple disappeared through one of four sets of tall double doors to the left of them. Mallory caught a glimpse of a sumptuous-looking dining room and sucked in her breath.

What a fantastic place to be raised! And paradise to have the Atlantic at your feet too?

Still mesmerized by such splendor, she didn't realize anyone else had entered the massive foyer until she heard a girl's voice cry, "Tia Lianor!"

Mallory turned around to discover two dark-haired girls around ten or eleven who'd come through double doors on the opposite side of the great hall. Behind them she saw a room with a counter and several people working. For a front desk, it had been cleverly hidden.

The girl who was staring at Mallory with brown eyes identical to Lianor's made a funny sound and put a hand to her mouth. The other girl holding something in her hand started to giggle.

"Are you Apolonia?"

The girl hesitated for a moment, then nodded.

"Do you speak English?" Mallory asked, drawing closer to them.

"Yes."

"I've heard lovely things about you from your Tia Lianor."

That brought a smile to the girl's face.

"She'll be down in a minute. My name is Mallory Ellis." She extended her hand.

"How do you do," Apolonia said in very proper English and shook it. Some flicker of recognition caused her features to become even more expressive. "You are her friend from California in America."

Friend. That was nice to hear.

"Yes. I've come to visit her for a couple of days. When you saw me from the back, you thought I was your aunt, didn't you?" Both

Mallory and Lianor happened to be wearing black pantsuits.

She nodded.

"Other people have said the same thing. Who's your friend?"

"Oh—" she cried, as if suddenly remembering her manners. "This is my best friend, Violente Camoes. We're waiting for her father."

Mallory grasped the other girl's hand that wasn't full of postcards. "It's a pleasure to meet you, Violente. I love your name."

"She does *not* like it," Apolonia confided. "Her brother says she was named after Queen Maria the First of Portugal. The servants called her Violente because she was *insano*."

"Insane?"

"Yes."

Trying to smother her laughter, Mallory said, "What's your brother's name, Violente?"

"Tomas."

"Ah—that explains it!"

"What do you mean?" Apolonia asked while both girls stared at her wide-eyed.

"Her brother is just jealous because he wasn't named after a king."

Apolonia turned to her friend and translated in Portuguese. Her friend's mouth broke into a wide smile. She whispered something back in Portuguese to Apolonia.

Mallory couldn't help but marvel at her grasp of English. Not only had she benefited from the English-speaking tourists who stayed here, according to Lianor her niece went to the same private school she'd once attended. It was run by the nuns. No wonder their family was so well educated.

"Violente thinks you're very nice. I do too."

"Well thank you. I feel the same way about both of you."

"My father said you are notarus."

Mallory blinked. "Do you mean notorious?"

"Yes. I don't know that word."

She choked down more laughter. Wait till she told Lianor. "I think he got it mixed up with the word industrious. It means I like to work and use my brain.'' She tapped the side of her head so the girls would understand.

''But he frowned like this when he said it,'' she informed her before doing a great imitation of one.

''*Violente?*''

At the sound of a male voice, all three of them turned in time to see a well-dressed man around forty enter the foyer. He signaled for his daughter to come. She waved goodbye to them, then ran toward him.

No sooner had they left the foyer than Lianor appeared on the stairs. Apolonia rushed toward her aunt and started talking in rapid Portuguese.

''Why don't you speak English in front of our guest. It will be good practice for you.''

''She already has. Very beautifully I might add,'' Mallory said after catching up with them. ''In fact I found out something quite interesting.''

Quickly she related her exchange with Apolonia. Lianor fought not to laugh in front of her niece. ''Your father's English is excellent, Apolonia, but sometimes even he makes mistakes.''

Mallory's gaze rested on the girl. ''I can't imagine being able to speak fluent Portuguese when I was your age. You have superior intelligence just like your aunt.''

Her sweet face lit up. ''Thank you.''

''Come with us,'' Lianor urged. ''We'll show you to your room.''

Mallory followed them to the second floor. The staircase curved around, giving out on a corridor that ran the length of the palace. In between paintings and tapestries, she glimpsed double doors to the various rooms.

They passed another exquisitely shaped marble staircase before reaching a pair of double doors facing them at the south end. They looked massive and impregnable.

Behind them was another set of doors. Above those she saw an inscription set in the colorful azulejo tiles for which Portugal was famous.

''What does it say?''

''*Our lips easily meet high across the narrow street.* It's a saying of the poet Frederico de Brito who wrote about the Alfama district of Lisbon where the streets between the houses are only four feet wide. The people on opposite sides can reach out of their homes and touch each other.''

Lianor rolled her eyes. "Someone in the D'Afonso family who had romantic notions put it there. Most likely it was a man who wanted to remind his wife of her marital duty,'' she muttered sotto voce.

"No doubt,'' Mallory concurred with a grin. She looked down at Apolonia who couldn't quite follow their whole conversation. Wanting to include her she said, "Why are there two sets of double doors?''

"This is where the king stayed. He kept soldiers by both doors.''

"If we're talking about Pedro II, I can see why,'' Mallory murmured. "The man must have had some serious enemies.''

Lianor's eyes met hers and they both chuckled. But Mallory's laughter ceased the moment she stepped inside the suite and got her first look at the royal apartment which was really a small palace within a palace.

The melange of Muslim, Arabic, Visigoth and Moorish accoutrements filling the huge rooms defied description.

Both D'Afonsos took her on the grand tour which included a living room with a priceless Moorish tile floor put down in bands of blue and white that undulated like the rolling waves across an ocean. Dark crisscrossed beams defined the painted ceiling of flowers and angels.

There was a library worth a king's ransom, a delightful airy music room with an antique piano, a sitting room, another bedroom, a kitchen and dining room which faced west and opened on to a private balcony that overlooked the ocean.

Lianor had to drag Mallory away from the view in order to show her the superb bedroom with its giant canopied bed and private balcony. It gave out on an unparalleled vista of the beach and ocean to the southwest. The constant crash of waves upon the sand far below set the rhythm of her heart. She felt enchanted.

Throwing back her head, she stood there breathing in the sea air while her long hair swished around her in the night breeze.

"Do you like it?" Apolonia asked.

Almost too enthralled to speak, she finally answered the girl's question.

"I love it so much, I think I shall sleep out here tonight in that lounger next to the table and dream."

"What will you dream about?

"Portuguese navigators who bravely set sail across the ocean to explore new worlds."

Apolonia looked delighted with that answer. "I love the ocean too."

"Living here, how could you not?"

"Do you like to swim?"

"It's my favorite sport."

"Mine too. My father taught me."

"Speaking of your father," Lianor broke in, "I bet he's looking for you."

She shook her head. "He went to see Maria in the hospital. I hope he says she can come home tomorrow."

A signal of distress passed from Lianor to Mallory.

"I'm sure he's back by now so you can ask him. It's getting late and I think everyone's tired, especially Mallory. She's flown all the way from New York.''

She put her arm around her niece's shoulders. ''Let's go to bed, shall we?''

The three of them walked to the first set of doors. Lianor turned to Mallory. ''What time do you want breakfast served in here?''

Knowing it wouldn't do any good to tell her not to go to the trouble she said, ''How about ten o'clock after my morning swim? But only if you and Apolonia join me.''

''We'll be here.''

Apolonia looked up at her. ''Do you like salsicha?''

''It's Portuguese sausage,'' Lianor supplied.

''Is that your favorite?''

''Yes.''

''Then I'll definitely try it. Good night, Apolonia.'' They hugged again. What a wonderful girl she was. If Mallory had a daughter, she'd want her to be exactly like Lianor's niece.

''Good night.''

''See you tomorrow,'' Lianor whispered.

Mallory nodded. ''Thank you for every-thing.''

''You're welcome.''

She closed the doors after them. When she turned around, she felt like she'd been magi-cally transported back in time. Phoenicians, Greeks, Romans, Moors had occupied this land. It was from these shores Vasco de Gama had set out on his voyage. Shivers of excite-ment raced through her body.

After she'd prepared for bed and left a voice message on her parents' phone to let them know she'd arrived safely, she walked out on the balcony with a pillow and blanket.

Mallory hadn't intended to sleep out there all night. But when she heard the sound of gulls and opened her eyes, light filled the sky and was burning off the morning mist. It looked like it was going to be a beautiful day.

She went inside and made hot chocolate, then took the colorful ceramic mug and walked back to the balcony where she watched the ocean for at least an hour. Every now and again she saw a ship in the far distance.

From her vantage point, the swells looked mild this morning. There were two curls of waves that broke some distance from the shore.

A few guests were already swimming, but they stayed close in. Several palace employees were arranging loungers, towels and umbrellas. The sandy beach was starting to show signs of life as more guests appeared. Mallory could hardly wait to get out there herself. She had time. Breakfast wouldn't be for another forty-five minutes.

Before leaving her condo in Los Angeles, she'd packed her ancient one-piece yellow and orange suit she always wore for surfing. She'd also brought a pair of sandals she wore on the beach. Once she was ready, she hurried out of the room and used the closest staircase to reach the ground floor.

"Bom Dia." A male palace employee opened the doors for her so she could go outside.

"Bom Dia," she answered. "Thank you."

The ocean was calling to her. After negotiating more steps down to the pristine beach, she stopped by the nearest lounger, deposited her sandals and ran into the water.

It was warmer than the ocean at Huntington Beach this time of day. Lianor had referred to this area as the Sun Coast where you could swim year-round.

This was heaven!

Mallory used the momentum from the fairly strong rip current to reach the curls quickly. In the late afternoon she would ask for a surf-board and come out again when the waves were bigger. Right now they were perfect for body surfing.

Once she got way out, she had so much fun she lost track of time. It wasn't until she was waiting for one final wave before going back to the palacio that she heard people shouting. The sounds of terrified voices made her suddenly aware of her surroundings.

There were at least twenty people gathered near the water. Amid all the noise she heard someone crying out Apolonia's name over and over again hysterically.

Oh no…

Mallory started swimming parallel to the shore, cleaving the water as fast as she could in the direction they were pointing. Several swimmers were making an attempt to get beyond the first curl, but they weren't strong enough.

A little further now she could see Apolonia who'd somehow made it past both curls, but she must have grown tired.

Her head was back, mouth open. Those little arms were extended, making downward motions in the water. She was drowning!

Please God. Don't let it happen.

In a few more strokes Mallory executed a deep dive under Apolonia, then came up behind her and put her hand under her chin.

''I'm here, darling. Lie still and let me do the work. Your father wouldn't want to go on living without you. I'll get you back to him,'' she promised.

Using the rescue side stroke, Mallory headed for shore with her precious cargo, praying all the way.

The crowd gathered round as she pulled the girl's limp body onto the beach and turned her on her side to get any water out of her lungs.

Though she felt a pulse, waves of fear washed over Mallory to realize Apolonia wasn't breathing. In an instant she put the girl on her back and immediately began mouth to mouth resuscitation.

Keep calm, Mallory. Pace yourself. Fifteen compressions, two ventilations. Fifteen compressions, two ventilations.

Time had no meaning as she settled down to perform this procedure for as long as it took. She'd only rescued one other person when she'd been out surfing. It was an adult who'd gotten in trouble, but after she'd reached the beach with him, he'd started breathing right away.

This was much different. Apolonia had been struggling too long. She had to live. There'd been enough tragedy in their household. She was exceptional. Her family needed her.

Let her live.

When Mallory had all but lost hope, she heard sputtering and quickly rolled Apolonia on her side to get rid of more water.

"Papa," the girl half moaned her father's name.

Mallory's heart rejoiced.

"I'm right here, *querida*," came a deep masculine voice so full of love and emotion, Mallory's eyes flooded with tears.

"We'll take over now," another voice sounded.

With exquisite relief, Mallory sat back on her heels to let the paramedics deal with Apolonia. Over the shoulders of one of them, her eyes met another pair of eyes. Intensely black and moist. They stared at her incredulously before the man got to his feet.

It had only been a fleeting moment of contact, yet she felt a trembling in her soul even after he'd followed the stretcher into the ambulance and it had driven off.

Lianor knelt down and wrapped her arms around Mallory, sobbing quietly as she poured out her gratitude. They stayed in that position until Mallory stopped trembling.

When they both finally got to their feet, an older woman standing nearby made the sign of the cross and kept murmuring something Mallory didn't understand. Lianor introduced them.

''This is our housekeeper, Ines. She's saying 'Bless you.'''

Mallory swallowed hard. ''Tell Ines that God helped me.''

After hearing the translation, the older woman's eyes filled with tears. They spilled down her pale cheeks.

The dozen or so sober-faced staff hovering next to the housekeeper said the same words, 'Bless you,' before they dispersed and got back to their duties. Ines followed them inside the palace.

Before resuming their various pleasures, the guests who'd been out on the beach congregated around Mallory and praised her in several languages for her heroic rescue.

That left one young woman in a bikini who looked to be in her late teens. She stood there with her face in her hands, weeping. Lianor went over and put her arm around her shoulders to comfort her.

"This is Brianca, Mallory. Just this morning Ines asked her to keep an eye on Apolonia until we had breakfast. They came down to swim. When my niece saw you body surfing, she wanted to do it too and slipped away before Brianca could stop her.

"The lifeguard doesn't come on duty until eleven o'clock, and Apolonia knows better than to go swimming without Rafael. As you can see, Brianca is devastated. I've tried to tell her it's not her fault."

No. The fault is mine.

Inhaling deeply, Mallory said, "Will you translate for me again, Lianor?"

"Of course."

"Tell Brianca I'm the one to blame. Last night Apolonia found out I love to swim. I'm positive she thought I'd seen her, and that's why she dared to venture past the curls. Ask Brianca if she was the one who called out Apolonia's name to me."

Lianor conveyed her wishes. Once Brianca understood what Mallory had been saying, she lifted her head and nodded.

"Remind her that she was the one who saved Apolonia's life. I was so busy having a marvelous time out there, I would never have known what was happening if I hadn't heard her screaming your niece's name in a clear voice."

More conversation ensued.

The teenager's face brightened a little.

"Tell her we need to be thankful that everyone did their part. The ambulance came just in time and everything worked out. I know Apolonia's going to be fine."

Again Lianor translated, but the teen still didn't seem totally convinced.

On impulse, Mallory hugged Brianca who hugged her back. They both shed a few more tears, then parted with smiles.

"Thank you," Brianca said in English before darting back to the palace.

As she ran off, Lianor squeezed Mallory's arm. "After receiving blame from everyone, especially from Ines who told my brother

Brianca could be trusted, she needed your kindness. You're a truly wonderful person, Mallory.''

''Please don't give me any credit. The only thing of importance is that Apolonia's alive. Where did the ambulance take her?''

''To the local hospital in Atalaia where Violente lives. It's five kilometers from here.''

''I want to see her.''

''We'll go after you've had breakfast and relaxed for a little while. I know you're strong, but that was an emotional as well as physical ordeal you've just been through. I don't want you passing out on me.''

They walked up the beach. Mallory picked up her sandals but didn't bother to put them on. ''There's no chance of that happening; however I must admit I could use some tea.''

''Come on. Let's go up to your room and take care of you.''

Side by side they hurried into the palace where Mallory took a shower and washed her hair. Since they were going to the hospital, she opted to wear a cotton blouse and matching wraparound skirt in a khaki tone.

When she entered the dining room and saw the amazing breakfast waiting for her, her appetite returned. Lianor was hungry too. They ate a little bit of everything including the sausage which had been cooked with green pepper, onion and a cheese sauce.

"Oh that's good. No wonder it's Apolonia's favorite."

Lianor's eyes filmed over. "Thanks to you, she'll be eating more of it, although she shouldn't," she added in a tremulous voice.

"What do you mean?"

"Apolonia has been putting on weight and looks like I did at her age, but Maria has never worried about things like that. Neither did my mother who fed us constantly. By the time I was seventeen, I was huge."

"I was overweight in my early teens too, but then I shot up and that changed everything."

"It didn't happen that way for me." As if she were embarrassed by the admission, she got up from the table. "How long do you think Apolonia will have to stay in the hospital?"

Lianor had changed the subject so fast, Mallory realised she'd just had a glimpse of the pain she hid from the world. Maybe one day she'd trust Mallory enough to tell her the rest.

"I have no idea. Every case is different. Maybe she'll be home by tonight."

"I hope so."

Mallory eyed her with concern. "I'm ready to go whenever you are." In truth she was anxious to see Apolonia for herself. There could be complications, but she hadn't wanted to upset her friend further by discussing them.

"I'll pack a bag for Apolonia and meet you at the car."

Within fifteen minutes they'd reached the hospital in the peaceful little town surrounded by beaches. Though not big, the hospital was as modern and up to date as any in Los Angeles.

After learning that Apolonia had been transferred from the ER to a private room, they walked to the nursing station on the main floor where Lianor found out which room down the hall was her niece's.

Mallory touched her arm. ''You go in first. You and your brother need some time alone with her. I'll wait in the lounge we passed.''

''Thanks. I won't be long.''

Once she was on her own, Mallory walked the short distance to the waiting room where she saw a mother nursing her baby in one corner, an old couple sitting in another holding hands. Mallory smiled at everyone and sat down.

Tension kept her body from relaxing. Until she knew how Apolonia was faring, she wouldn't have any peace. Not able to sit still, she got up and decided to take a walk outside. On the way to the exit she told the nurse at the desk she'd be right back.

The beautiful sunny day mocked the turmoil going on inside of her. Though she looked out on a calm ocean, all she saw was a pair of fathomless black eyes staring at her with a mixture of agony to think it might have claimed his daughter…and shock to think the woman he'd disliked without ever having met her, had plucked his Apolonia from its watery grasp in time to save her.

"Ms. Ellis?"

Mallory had heard that low, gravelly male voice earlier today. With heart pounding, she turned around.

She'd only noticed his eyes before.

Now she saw the whole man dressed in black swimming trunks and a blue T-shirt. He must have been planning to join his daughter in the surf when he'd heard she was in trouble.

Physically she saw nothing that nature could improve upon. His Mediterranean heritage gave him his olive skin. The arrangement of striking male features beneath vibrant black hair and brows created someone fascinating as well as unbelievingly appealing.

He had height and breadth in perfect proportion to his long powerful legs. Such an unforgettable face and strong, cut body could well inspire any artist to immortalize him on canvas.

To say he was an incredible-looking man would be an understatement.

"How's your daughter?" she asked tremulously.

She heard the ragged breath he took. "Right now they're giving Apolonia warmed fluids intravenously. So far she's holding her own. The doctor says if she doesn't develop additional symptoms in the next five hours, she'll be able to go home."

"That's wonderful news!" she cried. Mallory couldn't have been more thrilled if Apolonia were her own flesh and blood.

Those black eyes, eloquent with emotion, bore into hers. "You saved my daughter from drowning," his voice shook. "How does one person thank another for the gift of life?"

Mallory could hardly breathe. "You just did," she said in a quiet tone. "Would it help if I told you a lifeguard once saved *my* life when I was about Apolonia's age and thought the ocean was my friend?"

His eyelids closed tightly for a moment. Perhaps he was thinking Mallory's thoughts. That if she'd died, she wouldn't have been here to save his daughter.

But Mallory knew that if she hadn't come to Portugal, Apolonia wouldn't have gotten into trouble in the first place.

"A big part of our thanks needs to go to Brianca. She screamed your daughter's name loud enough for me to hear, and she kept screaming until she got my attention. That enabled me to return the favor the lifeguard did for me and my family by reaching Apolonia in time."

His features hardened. "Another few seconds in that water and she would have drowned," he whispered, still reliving the agony.

"But she didn't," Mallory said gently. "Seeing you like this, I now know what terror my parents must have experienced when the CPR didn't seem to be working on me. I was their only child too."

"Por Deus." His dark head reared back in more anguish. "I told her I would swim with her this morning. But she left my room before I did because I received a call from one of my hotel managers in Cabo Espichel I had to take.

"I was still talking to him in my bedroom upstairs when one of the maids burst in and told me to come quick. By the time I reached the beach, you were already giving her CPR."

He paused. "I've only known pain like that once before..."

Mallory knew he was talking about his wife. If she could steer his mind away from the worst—

After a slight pause, "I met your daughter last night. She's very precious."

A visible tremor passed through his body. He cleared his throat. "She hasn't stopped talking about you. When Lianor walked in the hospital room alone a few minutes ago, Apolonia begged me to come and find you."

Mallory bowed her head. "Will the doctor allow her to have visitors yet?"

"Only if it's the woman who restored my daughter to me. He feels it will aid in her recovery. So do I," he said in a husky tone.

CHAPTER THREE

MALLORY felt Rafael's hand on her waist, urging her forward. The touch was purely impersonal, but its warmth seeped through her body.

They went back inside the hospital and walked past the nursing station to Apolonia's room.

"You look terrific already," Mallory said to the ten-year-old after she reached her side. An answering smile greeted her. She was still being fed intravenously. "How do you feel?"

"Good. I want to go home."

"I don't blame you. Just give it a little more time and you'll be able to."

"Thank you for saving me." Moisture filled her brown eyes and ran out of the corners. "I tried to reach you, but I got tired." Her bottom lip quivered.

"I know, darling." Moved to tears, Mallory leaned over and kissed her cheek. Her color was coming back. ''Don't think about it any-more.''

''Will you take me swimming with you next time?''

Whoever said children were resilient knew what they were talking about. However there wouldn't be a next time. Mallory would be gone tomorrow, but Apolonia didn't need to hear anything that might slow her recovery over the next few hours.

''That's up to your father. For now you need to rest and get your strength back.''

She glanced at Rafael. ''When I'm better, can I body surf with Mallory?''

''I can't think of anyone I'd trust more,'' came his emotion-laden response.

''Thank you, Papa. I don't think you should tell Maria what happened to me. It would make her cry.''

He smoothed the hair off her forehead. ''I agree, *querida*. She needs happy thoughts.''

One look at the anxious expression on his face and Mallory turned her head aside. With his daughter and her adopted grandmother in different hospitals, the man had too much on his plate at the moment.

In truth, Mallory was having difficulty fighting her emotions too. No doubt the urge to break down and have a good cry had to be a delayed reaction to the events of the morning. What if she'd reached Apolonia too late?

"Are you all right?" Rafael demanded from across the bed.

Mallory looked back at him. This time the jet black gaze fastened on her conveyed deep concern.

"I'm fine. Maybe a little tired, just like your daughter." She put a hand on Apolonia's arm. "You need your sleep, darling. I'll talk to you later."

"Don't go!" the girl cried as Mallory turned to leave.

Apolonia's plea tugged at her heart. Lianor stood at the end of the hospital bed with concern on her face. Mallory looked to her for help.

"Mallory's right, Apolonia. The doctor wants you to remain quiet. We won't be far away."

"No," Apolonia broke down crying. "Stay in here with me. Don't let Mallory leave, Papa."

It warmed Mallory's heart to think the girl didn't want her to go.

"Hush, *querida*. She's not going any place," he declared with more than a hint of steel in his voice.

Hating herself for having said anything to upset his daughter, Mallory sat down in one of the overstuffed chairs. Lianor found the other one and subsided into it.

Rafael remained at his daughter's side, soothing her with his hand, murmuring endearments. It was beautiful to watch.

Every so often a nurse came in to take Apolonia's vital signs. No sooner would she type information into the computer than a resident would enter the room to check on her. Mallory held her breath every time in the hope that he wouldn't tell them something was wrong.

Between catnaps Apolonia asked Mallory questions about what ten-year-old girls did in America for fun. They chatted back and forth.

At one point Lianor slipped out of the room long enough to bring her brother a meal. When she returned, he ate part of it without enthusiasm. Who could blame him when his daughter's life hung in the balance?

Around six in the evening, Violente's dark-haired father stepped in the room. He walked over to the bed to talk to Rafael and give Apolonia a kiss. After a few minutes conversation he approached Lianor, but his eyes focused on Mallory.

Once introductions were made he said in English, "For a moment last night I thought you were Lianor."

"When she was in Los Angeles, some of the staff made the mistake of thinking she was me from a distance. I enjoyed meeting your daughter. Violente's a darling girl, Senhor Camoes."

"Please, call me Luis. She was certainly impressed with you." He studied the two of them. "Up close there is a difference, but both of you are beautiful." His eyes were alive with male admiration.

"Thank you," she and Lianor said at the same time.

"I hope you're here for a long stay."

"Much as I'd love to vacation here, I'll have to return to the States soon."

He smiled. "Not if Apolonia and my daughter have anything to say about it. News of your heroic rescue is the talk of Atalaia. My wife and I are hoping all of you will be our guests for dinner one evening when Apolonia's recovered. Carolina would be here now, but our baby is cutting teeth and is miserable."

"The poor little thing," Mallory murmured. "If I'm still at the palacio, that would be lovely."

"Good. We'll plan on it. *Boa noite.*"

"*Boa noite,*" Mallory responded, trying to imitate the accent.

Rafael had been standing close by and walked out with him. A few minutes later he came back followed by the kitchen staff with dinner trays for all them.

Mallory looked at her food, but couldn't eat. She had no appetite. Neither did Lianor.

When she thought she couldn't stand the suspense any longer, the doctor swept in. He smiled at everyone and spoke in Portuguese to Rafael for a moment. After they'd conversed, he suddenly switched to accented English.

"I was just telling Rafael that it appears our patient has done extremely well." He listened to her heart and lungs, felt her pulse.

"I don't want to stay here anymore," Apolonia complained to him.

"Just as soon as the nurse comes in to take out the IV, you won't have to. I'm releasing you."

Mallory's heart leaped for joy. "Thank God," she heard Rafael whisper. Lianor grasped Mallory's arm. The relief everyone felt was positively tangible.

"But you have to obey my instructions when you get home," he insisted.

"I will."

"The first thing you must do is go straight to bed. Tomorrow if you feel strong enough, you can get up and dressed."

"When can I go swimming?"

He chuckled. "Give it at least three days. By then you should be feeling a hundred percent. All right?"

"But that's too long to wait! Mallory's leaving to go back to America tomorrow." The girl sounded panicked.

Mallory bowed her head, hating to be the source of Apolonia's agitation once again.

"She has changed her plans," Rafael stated unequivocally.

"Is that true?" Apolonia cried. Even Lianor looked stunned.

This was the second time Rafael had spoken for Mallory when it wasn't his place. She was beginning to understand Lianor's desire for independence where her brother was concerned. But now was not the time to take issue with him. She didn't have the heart to deny his daughter anything.

"Yes."

She would call Liz and explain what happened. The older woman had been urging Mallory to take a vacation. Six weeks if she wanted. In fact at one point she'd demanded it until Mallory had explained that she enjoyed her work and didn't relish the thought of taking a vacation alone.

Liz said she understood and the subject hadn't been broached again. Now it seemed Mallory had a compelling reason to stay in Portugal for a little while longer.

She thought she detected a gleam of satisfaction in Rafael's eyes before he walked out of the room with the doctor. Lianor said she would bring the car around to the entrance. That left Mallory alone with Apolonia.

After the nurse removed the IV and left, Mallory found a brush in the overnight bag. After getting the tangles out of Apolonia's hair, she put it in a French braid, securing it with an extra band Mallory always carried in her purse.

Apolonia beamed as she reached around with her hand and felt it. "I love it! Maria wouldn't let me wear braids."

"Why not?"

"She said if God wanted me to wear them, I would have been born with them."

Mallory had to stifle her laughter. "Well, maybe we can be forgiven this once since I'm a foreigner.'' She reached for the clothes in the case and helped her get dressed in pants, a cotton top and sandals.

''What a cute outfit!'' she said, lifting her back on the side of the bed where she could sit while they waited for her father.

''Tia Lianor picked it out for me.''

''She has good taste.''

''It doesn't make me look as fat.''

What?

''You're not fat.''

''Tomas says I am. So do some of the boys at school.'' She gazed at Mallory with tear-filled eyes.

Without conscious thought Mallory drew her close and hugged her. ''Your aunt tells me you resemble your mother. I understand she was a real beauty.

''Whenever your father looks at you, I'm sure he sees your mother in you. One day the boys will tell you you're beautiful just like she was. Wait and see.''

''I want to look like you and Tia,'' she cried quietly against Mallory's chest.

She rocked her back and forth, understanding her torment.

"I went through a plump phase in adolescence, Apolonia. Lots of girls and boys do."

Her head went back so she could look at her. "You?" Her innocent eyes had widened.

"Yes." It was hell trying to ignore the cruel remarks from boys. "I suffered a lot from their mean comments, but I eventually grew taller and thinner."

Apolonia smiled in spite of her tears. "I'm glad you came. I love you." She hugged her harder.

"I love you too," Mallory whispered against her temple, realizing it was true. After hearing about Lianor's struggle because of a weight problem, it appeared history was going to repeat itself if no one stepped in to prevent it from happening to Apolonia.

"I'm ready to go anytime you two are," a familiar male voice spoke up.

Mallory eased herself away from the girl's arms to face Rafael. No telling how long he'd been standing there with the nurse who'd brought in a wheelchair.

Aware of his scrutiny, Mallory averted her eyes and put the brush in the case on top of a robe and pajamas. Thank heaven Apolonia wouldn't be needing them here.

"I like your new hairdo, *querida.*"

"So do I, but we can't tell Maria."

"No. It will remain our secret. Let's go home."

Rafael gathered his daughter in his strong arms and lowered her into the wheelchair. The nurse took over and started to push her out of the room.

Apolonia looked over her shoulder. "Come on, Mallory."

She picked up the overnight bag. "I'm right behind you."

Rafael held the door open for her. "I hope you realize you've won my daughter's lifetime devotion."

Though no part of them was touching, they were so close she could feel the warmth of his body. In that millisecond she became sexually aware of him. Her body's involuntary reaction shocked her so much, she trembled.

"Apolonia won mine last night. She has enough charm to twist anyone around her little finger."

Rafael was thinking the same thing about the woman who walked past him on those long, shapely legs. A few minutes ago he'd watched Apolonia hug her in earnest.

Until his daughter had been miraculously rescued and brought back to life, Rafael hadn't thought Mallory could do anything to change his feelings toward her. But there was no getting around the fact that he owed a debt of gratitude to this woman he could never repay.

Months before this morning's horrific events, she'd made such an impact on Lianor, his sister had actually been prepared to have Mallory stay at her apartment.

Aside from the family and a few close friends like Joana, Lianor didn't normally allow other women to get that close to her, let alone men…

But right now too many unexpected emotions were bombarding him to think clearly about the ramifications of Mallory's advent into their lives. After Apolonia's brush with death, the worry over how she would deal with the loss of Maria was still plaguing him.

He held the outer doors of the hospital open for the nurse to push his daughter outside. Mallory walked behind them. Like Lianor, she was taller and more voluptuous than most of the women he knew.

"Thank you." She flashed him a brief glance.

In a country filled with dark-eyed people, the brilliance of her indigo blue eyes caught him off guard.

"De nada," he whispered, assailed for the moment by the faint scent of roses wafting past him.

Lianor stood by the car, waiting. When she saw them, she reached for the suitcase and put it in the trunk. Mallory got in front with her.

Rafael climbed in the back seat, then reached for his daughter and pulled her onto his lap. He thanked the nurse for her help before she closed the door and waved them off.

"Papa? Can I use your cell phone to call Violente?"

He kissed the top of his daughter's head. "I'm sorry but I didn't bring it with me, *querida*."

"I wanted to tell her what happened."

"Luis has already told her."

"You can use my phone," Lianor offered. "It's in my purse. Mallory? Would you get it out?

"Of course." After a moment she turned around in the seat. "Here you go, Apolonia."

"Thank you," she said after taking it from her.

In that instant before Mallory faced forward again, her gaze collided with Rafael's. Again he had the sensation of being caught in a force field of electric blue light.

Judging by the conversation in Portuguese his daughter held with her best friend during the short drive home, other forces seemed to be at work as well. Her assertions that she loved Mallory and wished she would never leave Portugal sounded so heartfelt, it shook him.

Apolonia didn't need anything else to rock her world, not when Maria's death was a foregone conclusion.

"Will you come to my room please?" Apolonia asked Mallory after they'd all gotten out of the car.

"She can't, *querida*," Rafael intervened. "After rescuing you this morning, she needs her rest too." He'd been worried about Mallory who had to be exhausted in more ways than one after the harrowing experience in the ocean.

Lianor backed him up. "Your father's right. In fact we could all use a good night's sleep." She got the overnight bag out of the trunk.

"I'll have breakfast with you in the morning," Mallory promised. "The one we should have had *this* morning." She winked before giving her a kiss on the cheek. Rafael felt the impact of that wink in parts of him he didn't know were there. "What time do you usually eat?"

"We'll expect you at eight," he answered before his daughter could speak. "I'll send

Nina to show you where to come. *Boa noite,* Mallory.''

She flicked him another brief regard. *''Boa noite.''*

Conflicted by the deepest feelings of gratitude for this woman who represented the type of female he couldn't abide, he picked up his cherub and started for the stairs leading to the private entrance to the palacio. Lianor accompanied him.

''Good night!'' Apolonia called out to Mallory. ''Thank you for saving me!''

Amen, Rafael said inwardly, hugging his child closer.

Mallory had already started for the main entrance. She turned and waved. The soft breeze coming off the ocean swirled her long, dark brown hair around her shoulders.

Unable to help himself, his veiled gaze dropped lower to where the breeze molded the material of her clothes against her enticing curves. He felt stirrings inside of him he didn't want to feel.

Not for this particular woman.

Ines welcomed Apolonia with a happy cry. Her reaction distracted him briefly from recurrent thoughts of Mallory he couldn't seem to control on his own.

The housekeeper followed the three of them to his daughter's bedroom on the upper floor. She left a tray with apple juice and rolls on the bedside table.

Between the food and conversation, all of it centered on Mallory, Apolonia was finally ready to climb under the covers and go to sleep. When he was satisfied she wouldn't wake up, he motioned for Lianor to come into his room through the connecting door. He decided to leave it ajar in case Apolonia cried out for him in the night.

Once he was alone with his sister he said, ''We have to talk.''

''I agree. Apolonia's too vulnerable right now to hear bad news about Maria. I'm thinking this would be the best time to make the replacement. Someone who could start tomorrow and be here for her. It will help take away the sting when the end comes for Maria.''

"I knew I could count on you, Lianor." He reached for his sister and rocked her back and forth. "Apolonia has never needed you more than now. Tomorrow you can tell Mallory you're resigning. While she's still here in Portugal, she'll be able to interview the other staff at the shop and promote one of them to manager."

To his surprise she pulled away from him.

"You've misunderstood, Rafael. I didn't mean *me*."

His spirits plummeted. He shook his head in disbelief. "What are you saying?"

"That I have a career just like you. One I love. I'm not about to give it up. I was talking about Joana."

Joana—

"She's divorced and back home from Spain needing to make a new life. She and Apolonia have always liked each other. It would be perfect."

Rafael was barely holding on to his control. "There's all the difference between like and love, Lianor," he bit out. "And that's only the tip of the iceberg. A recently divorced woman has too many problems of her own.''

''Oh for heaven sakes, Rafael. Do you have any idea how you sound?''

''I've dated several divorcées, and trust me...I know what I'm talking about. My daughter needs—''

''Someone perfect?''

His head reared back.

''Guess what, Rafael—there isn't such a person. At the moment you think no one could replace Maria, and you'd be right. No one will ever be able to fill her particular shoes.

''But Joana is a loving person from one of the best families. She has known Apolonia since she was born. When Maria dies, she'll be there to lean on. At this stage in your daughter's life, it would be good for her to depend on someone she knows, someone who's younger, yet mature enough to see her through the teenage years.''

''This is a pointless conversation, Lianor. Joana would never make it that far. Her ex-husband will probably cause her trouble for the rest of their lives. The last thing I want is for

Apolonia to be involved in that emotional morass.

"More importantly, I don't want an outsider involved in our family's business. Maria might not be blood, but she was there from the beginning. It's the same thing."

His sister's chin jutted. "By placing those parameters on the situation, it looks like you'll have to find yourself a wife! Maybe it's time you practiced what you preach. *Boa noite,* Rafael."

Lianor left his suite by the door to the main corridor. He would have called her back, but he feared it would waken Apolonia.

Better to continue this conversation in the morning when they were both fresh. He wasn't through with his sister. She thought she might have had the last word, but tomorrow he would ask her to visit Maria with him. He'd come up with as many plans as it took until she caved.

Afraid he wouldn't get any sleep tonight, he wandered out on the balcony, but one look at the ocean reminded him he could have lost Apolonia today.

The haunting memory of her white face, of Mallory giving her the breath of life—

He closed his eyes tightly, wondering if his mind would always see that picture and cause his heart to fail every time.

But then another memory took over. The one where he heard Apolonia say his name and he realized Mallory had been the angel who'd saved her from certain death. Without her, his daughter wouldn't be sleeping quietly in the adjoining room.

A moan escaped his throat.

Thank God for you, Mallory.

"Papa?"

He wheeled around in surprise. "*Querida?* Can't you sleep?"

She walked quietly toward him. Looking up into his eyes she said, "How soon is Maria going to die?"

Taut bands around his chest constricted his breathing. "Who told you about her?"

"I heard you and Tia Lianor talking."

He got down on his haunches and placed his hands on her shoulders. "I was going to tell you at breakfast this morning. I'm sorry you had to find out this way. The doctor said it won't be much longer.''

''Can I go see her at the hospital?'' She was fighting tears.

''Of course. As soon as you've had a few days rest.'' He pulled her into his arms.

She wound hers around his neck. ''Sometimes I've heard Maria say the pain was so bad she wanted to die. I want her to die, Papa. Then she won't hurt anymore because she'll be in heaven.''

Rafael lost his battle with tears. ''I want that too. She'll be able to rest, free of pain.''

''I'm glad.''

''My brave, brave girl,'' he whispered in a shaken voice.

Afraid she'd been out of bed too long, he carried her back to her room and tucked her in once more.

''Papa?''

''Yes, *querida?*'' He sat down next to her, smoothing the strands of hair from her forehead.

''I'm glad you're not going to ask Joana to take care of me.''

It appeared his daughter had overheard a great deal of the conversation with his sister.

"As if I would. I know there's only one person you want, and that's your Tia Lianor."

She shook her head solemnly. "No I don't."

He was stunned. "I realize you think you're big enough to be here alone when I'm away on business. However Ines has her own duties, and we can't rely on Violente's mother. You need your aunt. She loves you and will watch over you when I can't."

"But Tia Lianor doesn't like it at the palacio."

Her comment couldn't have shocked him more. "Did she tell you that?"

"Yes."

"When?"

"A long time ago. She said there were too many bad memories here. Why was she unhappy, Papa?"

He expelled a troubled sigh. "She fell in love with someone who worked for the family, but he went away. It broke her heart."

There was a lot more to it than that, but his daughter didn't need to know all the ugly details.

"When she let me and Violente sleep over at her apartment last week, she said she was happy. I think she feels better now."

With that revelation Rafael got to his feet.

"If she met the right man, she'd be happy to come home again. She loves you like her own daughter."

"I know. But until that happens, do you think Mallory would stay with me?"

Rafael didn't know whether to laugh or cry.

"Apolonia— Mallory is the vice president of a corporation in America. She has great responsibilities."

"She could quit."

"No, *querida.*"

"Why not?"

"Mallory's a brilliant career woman who will probably own her own conglomerate one day. She's married to her work."

"You can't marry your work. You're silly, Papa."

He rubbed his hand over his face. "What I meant was, she loves her work the way I love mine."

"Do you love it more than me?"

"Never!" He sank down next to her and kissed her cheeks. "I love you so much, I couldn't comprehend life without you. Today when I thought you weren't going to wake up..." Rafael couldn't go on talking.

"I love you too, Papa. Do you want to know what Mallory told me?"

He was almost afraid to ask. "What?"

"When she grabbed me in the water, she said you loved me more than life, and if I did what she told me, she would get me back to you safely. All I had to do was stay calm and she would do the rest."

His daughter's soul shone from her eyes. "She's so brave and kind. And she's fun! Violente thinks so too. I love her, Papa."

Tell me something I don't already know.

Needing a little inspiration about now Rafael said, "I understand why you feel the way you do. She saved your life. It's something you'll always remember. But she's not the motherly type and never will be. What you want isn't possible.''

''Are you still angry with her?''

''Angry—''

''Yes. I remember how upset you were when Tia Lianor took the manager job and flew to California.''

A groan escaped his throat. ''I'm not angry with Mallory, *querida*. How could I be after what happened today?''

His daughter gave him a sweet smile. ''Good,'' she murmured before closing her eyes and turning on her side. ''*Boa noite,* Papa.''

CHAPTER FOUR

WHEN Mallory heard a knock on the door, she glanced at her watch. It was only seven-fifteen a.m. Too early to be the maid.

"Liz? Someone's here. I'm going to have to hang up. Thank you for being so understanding about this. I'll book a flight to Los Angeles for Friday. Talk to you later." She hung up the phone.

"I'm coming! Just a minute!" Grabbing her robe to throw over the underwear she'd put on after her morning shower, she hurried to the door. But it wasn't Lianor standing on the other side.

"Apolonia—"

Rafael's daughter had dressed in jeans and a yellow knit top. To Mallory's relief, her color was back, attesting to a good night's sleep. No one would know she'd been in the hospital yesterday.

"Come in." She stepped inside. "Don't you look pretty this morning."

"Thank you. I wish I had a robe like that."

The flowing white affair with lace at the hem and sleeves was no doubt meant for a bride.

"It is lovely, isn't it. My mother gave it to me a few years ago. This is the first time I've worn it."

"You look beautiful."

Mallory hugged her. "You're a sweetheart. You must be feeling a lot better this morning."

The girl nodded. "I wanted to talk to you before breakfast. Is it all right?"

"Of course. Come in the bedroom. I was just about to put on an outfit like yours."

While Apolonia waited, Mallory discarded her robe and slipped on a pair of designer jeans and a short-sleeved cotton sweater in a periwinkle hue.

"There. Now I'm ready."

She extended her hand for Apolonia to clasp. Together they strolled out to the balcony. A mist still hugged the shore, but the temperature was delightful.

For a minute neither of them spoke as they contemplated the ocean. No matter what, she imagined Apolonia had some misgivings about going in it again.

"Why don't we stretch out on these loungers like ladies of leisure. That's how I feel. As if I'm a very spoiled queen living in a palace with nothing more to do than daydream my life away."

Within seconds they were lying on their backs, side by side.

"Did you have daydreams when you were ten?"

"Oh yes... All the time."

"Did you have a favorite"

"Absolutely," Mallory declared. "Don't you?"

"Yes."

"Can you tell me what it is?"

"After you tell me yours."

Mallory smiled. Growing up she'd tended the kids of her mother's friends. But none of them were as entertaining and intelligent as Apolonia.

For the next few minutes she related the story from the comic books about the Amazon women of Paradise Island with their special powers. "I wanted to be just like them."

"Are they beautiful too?"

"Very. When I get back to California, I'll send you a comic book. Your English is so good, you'll probably be able to understand most of it without your father helping you."

When Apolonia didn't say anything, Mallory turned toward her, alarmed that something might be wrong. At this juncture the girl was sitting up, eyeing her with an anxious expression.

"Darling? Are you all right?"

Apolonia bit her lip. "I'd like that comic book, but I wish you wouldn't go away. Now that Maria's going to die, do you think you could be my nanny?"

The astounding question posed with such simplicity and earnestness sent Mallory into shock.

She got up from the lounger wondering if she'd even heard the girl correctly.

In the first place, she didn't know Apolonia had been told about Maria's fatal condition. In the second, she was positive Rafael knew nothing about this, otherwise Apolonia wouldn't have stolen to Mallory's room this early to talk to her before the whole family had breakfast together.

"Tia Lianor got her heart broken here at the palacio," Apolonia explained in a wistful voice. "That's why she lives in Lisbon. She wants her friend Joana to take care of me, but Joana doesn't act like she likes me very much when Tia Lianor isn't there. And papa said he wouldn't let her come anyway because she just got divorced and has too many problems.

"Last night he and Tia Lianor had a fight. She got so mad she told him to go find himself a wife. But I'm afraid for him to get married because he might pick someone who doesn't like me." Apolonia's voice trembled.

"So I was thinking you could stay here and do your work on the phone and the computer just like papa does. We have so many rooms. I wouldn't cause any trouble while you're busy.

"And then when you're free, we could go swimming and take drives and explore new places. Don't you think that would be fun?

"When I'm in school, you would have all day to work. I'd come home and do my homework. If you had to go on a trip, Ines would take care of me if papa were out of town too."

Every word squeezed Mallory's heart a little more. What could she say to this vulnerable girl who was already feeling lost without Maria?

Something horribly traumatic must have happened in Lianor's life for her not to be taking an active role in helping raise her niece now. Since coming to Portugal, Mallory had assumed the other woman's desire to live an independent life had more to do with separating herself from her autocratic brother.

But Apolonia's explanation revealed that someone else other than Rafael was responsible for driving Lianor away from the only family she had left. The revelation changed Mallory's perspective about him as well as the whole situation.

Secretly Mallory agreed with him about Joana. A woman just coming out of a divorce needed a few years to get in touch with herself again before she took on the monumental task of caring for someone else's child.

Without Lianor's help, Rafael had to be feeling desperate. Mallory could understand that, especially if the memory of Isabell had prevented him from getting married again.

You didn't take another wife to give your child a mother she might not like, not if you weren't madly in love. Under those circumstances Mallory couldn't imagine a worse scenario for three people.

"Papa's not mad at you anymore."

A sound between a laugh and a cry worked its way out of Mallory. With her back still toward her she said, "Apolonia—does your father know you were going to ask me about this?"

"No. When I told him I wanted you to stay and take care of me, he said it was impossible because you're married to your work and one day you'll own a conglomer."

She blinked. "Conglomerate?"

"Yes. He said you aren't the motherly type and never will be. Is that true? Don't you want to have a baby someday like Violente's mother? He's so cute. Sometimes we watch him for her when she takes a nap and—"

"*Perdoa, senhora—*" one of the maids interrupted from the entry to the balcony. Her gaze flew to Apolonia. "Your father had a great fright when he couldn't find you in your bed. He has sent everyone looking for you."

Mallory had feared as much. "We're on our way to breakfast now," she assured the anxious woman who rushed off, visibly relieved. After yesterday's terrifying experience, Mallory imagined the staff didn't want to suffer through a repeat performance today.

"I'll show you where to go," Apolonia said as they left the suite and started down the long corridor to the center staircase. At the top she paused, staring up at Mallory with a look of defeat in her pain-filled brown eyes.

"Papa will be angry if he finds out I asked you to be my nanny. He said you wouldn't want to take care of me. When you see him, please don't tell him anything."

"Apolonia—wait—"

But she ran down the stairs, obviously hurt by Mallory's silence. *And* embarrassed.

Devastated to have caused her any grief, Mallory couldn't think about eating or anything else, not while she was still reeling from the revelation that Apolonia wanted her to take over Maria's role.

Her father had told his daughter it never could or would happen. He'd branded Mallory as hard and unmotherly.

She'd laughed before. Oddly enough she wasn't laughing now. Did Rafael honestly see her that way?

Certainly she'd never cared what the Jack Hendleys of the world thought. They knew nothing. But for Apolonia's father to still believe it after what they'd all lived through yesterday disturbed and angered her.

Mallory had a strong maternal instinct. Though she might be a woman who wanted to control things in a serious way, it didn't mean she wanted nothing else but a brilliant career out of life!

Like Rafael, she hadn't yet met anyone who could enrich the life she already enjoyed to the point that she wanted to get married. However that didn't rule out her hope that it would happen one day.

How dare he make assumptions like that? Particularly when Apolonia was such an endearing girl. Mallory had taken to her from their very first meeting. After begging God to save her life, she doubted she could have any stronger feelings for Apolonia if she were her own flesh and blood.

When Mallory reached the foyer, she came to a standstill. Rafael had just emerged from behind the doors of the front desk dressed in a formal suit. He looked so attractive her heart skipped a beat, but he was in such a rush he almost collided with his daughter.

Mallory moved toward them. There was something about the way he was holding on to Apolonia while he spoke to her. His grave demeanor was prompted by more than just the fear that he hadn't been able to find her.

Suddenly Apolonia burst into tears and clung to her father.

There was no doubt in Mallory's mind that Maria had passed away. This was verified when Lianor came out of the same door wearing a navy suit. She rushed over to Mallory, her face pale, her eyes red-rimmed.

''Maria died at the hospital twenty minutes ago,'' she whispered. ''We didn't think it would happen this fast! Rafael went into Apolonia's room to tell her, but she wasn't there.''

''She came to my room a little while ago.''

''I had a feeling she'd gone to see you, so I sent Nina. Thank goodness she found you two together or I don't think my brother could have handled any more emotional shocks. We have to drive to Lisbon to take care of all the arrangements. Apolonia needs to eat and get ready.''

''Surely she won't be able to see Maria before the funeral.''

''No, but Rafael is afraid Apolonia is too fragile right now to be left here with the staff.''

''I'll stay with her. You two go on.''

Lianor shook her head. ''Rafael would never allow it. You flew here on a business trip and ever since then, it's been one life and death situation after another. You'll wish you'd never come.''

''That's not true, Lianor.'' The reality of Maria's death had taken hold of her friend. And the family's situation had touched her heart. How hard for all of them. ''I'll speak to your brother myself.''

She had to run to catch up with him and Apolonia. They'd passed through the front desk area only to disappear behind another door. It led to a drawing room in their private residence. The decor was even more fabulous than that of the Alfama suite.

''Rafael—wait!'' She could hear Lianor's footsteps behind her.

He paused midstride and turned around. His black eyes met hers in stunned surprise that she'd followed them.

''Mallory?'' The lines of strain around his mouth made him look older.

''I'm so sorry to hear about Maria. Lianor tells me you have a lot of things to deal with today. Why don't you let me take care of Apolonia?''

His daughter's precious face brightened despite her tears. ''Please can I stay with her, Papa?'' she begged without hesitation.

Mallory could feel tension radiating from him. It was a war between what he knew was best for his daughter, and his reluctance to impose on Mallory whom he didn't consider nanny material under any circumstances.

''When Nina came to my suite looking for her, we were in the middle of a big conversation. Over breakfast we can finish the rest of it, then I'll make sure she rests.'' After a pause, ''Those were the doctor's orders,'' Mallory reminded him.

''Please, Papa?''

''She'll be safe with me, I swear it.''

''You think I don't know that?'' he ground out emotionally. Something flickered in the deep recesses of his eyes before she heard him expel a deep breath. ''If you're sure it won't be too much trouble, I'd be very grateful.''

''It will be my pleasure.'' Mallory reached for Apolonia's hand. She grasped it tightly.

''Thank you,'' Lianor murmured.

Rafael eyed his daughter, then Mallory. "We'll try not to be too long."

She met his sober gaze once more. "Don't worry about anything. We're going to be fine."

"Come on, Mallory. Our private dining room is this way." She started pulling her toward the far doors. Mallory felt his scrutiny on her retreating back all the way out.

"Do you always eat in here?" she asked once they were seated at the end of the banquet table. The huge room contained furniture to accommodate two dozen people at least.

"Yes." She swallowed her juice. "Do you like it?"

Mallory picked up a hot roll and buttered it. "It's magnificent, but now I know how two little mice feel when they come in from outside."

"You're funny," Apolonia said before they both made inroads on their sausage.

"My whole condo in Los Angeles could probably fit in one quarter of this room. I eat in a little breakfast nook off the kitchen. It can only hold two people comfortably."

That produced a smile. "I wish I could see it."

"You heard your papa at the hospital. He said he'd take you to America one day."

"Maybe we could fly back with you and all go to Disneyland together. Tia Lianor said I would love it."

"Everyone loves Disneyland." Mallory smiled. "I'd like to watch your father take a ride on the Matterhorn's roller coaster."

"Is it scary?"

"Yes."

"Papa's not scared of anything."

Except losing you.

"I think *you* would love Mr. Toad's Wild Ride."

Apolonia frowned. "I don't understand. What's a toad?"

"Like a frog?"

"Ew. What's 'wild'?"

Mallory made a crazy face. Her young companion laughed. "Have you ever heard the story of the Wind in The Willows?"

"No. Tell me!"

"Do you have a computer in your room?"

"No, but papa has one in his office. I play games on it sometimes."

Hopefully Rafael wouldn't mind her using it for a few minutes. "Are you through with breakfast?"

"Yes."

"So am I. Let's go in there and I'll try to find it online. Maybe it will show a picture of Mr. Toad."

After passing through another hallway, they came to his office which was more like a private study. To her surprise it was smaller and more modern than many of the other rooms.

She pulled up another chair to his desk so they could sit side by side. Near one corner she spied a five by seven picture of a beautiful raven-haired woman who could only be his wife. A smaller picture of Apolonia was propped next to it.

"Papa left the computer on."

"All right. Let's see…"

Mallory typed Wind in the Willows in the address bar. In a second up popped a dozen different possibilities. She clicked on the one with excerpts and pictures.

After scrolling down, "There's Mr. Toad getting dressed in a gown." While Apolonia studied the wonderful old drawing, Mallory gave her a thumbnail sketch of the story. "Here's the part about his wild ride.

"They piled on more coals, and the train shot into the tunnel, and the engine rushed and roared and rattled, till at last they shot out at the other end into fresh air and the peaceful moonlight, and saw the wood lying dark and helpful upon either side of the line. The driver shut off steam and put on brakes, the Toad got down on the step, and as the train slowed down to almost a walking pace he heard the driver call out, 'Now, jump!'"

Apolonia looked over at her. "I can't wait to go on that ride. Do you think there's a picture of the Amazon women on here too?"

"I'm sure there is."

Another couple of clicks and Apolonia was able to feast her eyes on the characters in the famous comic strip.

"What's she carrying?"

"A rope of gold called a lasso. When you put it around somebody, they have to tell the truth."

A broad smile broke out on her piquant face.

"Pretty exciting isn't it?" Mallory murmured.

"This one with blue eyes looks just like you."

"Don't I wish! Would you like to see my favorite Hollywood actor?"

"Yes! This is fun."

"I agree." In fact Mallory hadn't had this much fun in a long long time. "Okay…" She typed in some more words and clicked. "Ah. Here he is…the man of my dreams."

Up came pictures of Larry "Buster" Crabbe, the attractive Olympic swimmer who starred in the first serialized Flash Gordon movies. Apolonia looked closer. "Fl-a-sh," she sounded out the name. "What does flash mean?"

"Do you know the word 'lightning'?" She nodded. "That's what a flash is. See? He wears a bolt of lightning on his costume. He got his name because he was powerful and quick and his enemies couldn't catch him. He was my heartthrob.''

''Heartthrob?''

''My heart beats fast just thinking about him.''

Apolonia's mouth curved upward. ''He has the blondest hair I've ever seen!''

''It's curly too.'' Mallory winked at her. ''I always wanted to marry him.''

''Do you still?''

Mallory chuckled. Kids... ''If he were available, I'd be his wife in a shot.''

''In a shot?''

''Right this minute.''

''Are you telling a joke?''

''Not at all. Did you have a favorite movie or book when you were little?'' Apolonia nodded. ''Why don't you type in the title and see what comes up?''

In a second a whole list of books appeared in Portuguese, but there were no pictures. ''This one.'' She tapped on the screen.

''What does the title mean?''

''Rose, My Pink Sister.''

"That sounds interesting. Why don't you tell me the story while we go upstairs? I want to see what your room looks like." Whether Apolonia felt tired or not, Mallory thought it best if she napped for a while.

After she'd closed all the windows on the computer, they left the study and went up another staircase. Apolonia entertained her with the charming tale all the way to the bedroom.

Although the bedroom was large, Mallory could see it had been modernized. Everything was very feminine with a tiny blue and yellow flowered print on the walls and matching quilts on the two double beds.

"I like it in here," she exclaimed. There was an armoire, and a dresser covered with stuffed animals and dolls. A charming antique dressing table with lamps rested against another wall.

Next to it was a breakfront filled with all kinds of games and toys. She also had a writing desk. Above it were shelves filled with books.

"The closet and bathroom are in there." Apolonia pointed to a set of double doors on one side of the room. ''Papa's room is through those others.''

A vision of Rafael D'Afonso lounging in his bed flashed into her mind. Disturbed by the intimate picture and how breathless it made her feel she said, ''Did Maria sleep in here?''

''No,'' she answered quietly. ''Her bedroom is across the hall.''

Mallory took off her sandals and lay back on the bed that hadn't been made up yet. She turned and propped her head in her hand.

''Why don't you lie down and tell me about Maria. What did you like best about her?''

To her relief Apolonia removed her tennis shoes and climbed under her covers. Soon the girl was painting a picture of her life for Mallory. She had a lot to say. Mallory let her talk and listened to her cry.

When there was a cessation of tears Mallory said, ''Maria sounds so wonderful, I think you should write everything down and make a book about her. Some day when you're married and have children, they'll ask you what your life was like with Maria. You can read it to them.''

Apolonia sat up in her bed. "Will you help me with it?"

"Of course. Why don't we start on it this afternoon after lunch. I bet you have a lot of pictures of her."

She nodded. "And in her room there are photos of her when she was a little girl with her family. We could put those in it too!" Apolonia sounded excited.

"Did she have a favorite flower?"

"Once papa gave her white roses for her birthday and she cried."

"Then we'll buy some for you to put on her grave. You could press one in your book for a memento."

After a long silence she whispered, "I love you."

"I feel the same way about you, darling."

Mallory sensed Apolonia wanted to say something else, then held back, but Mallory knew what it was. In truth, she hadn't been able to think of anything else since Apolonia had asked if she would be her nanny. In a few more minutes the girl turned on her stomach and quiet reigned.

When Mallory could tell she was asleep from physical and emotional exhaustion, she got up and went to one of the sets of windows overlooking the ocean. A restlessness had taken hold of her. She wished the room had a balcony.

What *was* Rafael going to do about his daughter?

Maybe if Mallory took Lianor aside and told her it would fine if she had to resign from Lady Windemere for Apolonia's sake— Perhaps her friend needed to hear that from Mallory so she wouldn't feel any guilt about leaving the company.

But if Lianor was so scarred she couldn't bring herself to live at the palacio with all its attendant memories, then it wouldn't help the situation and might even upset Lianor more.

Any way you looked at it, their family was going to be facing a horribly difficult transition period. She imagined it would take weeks if not several months while Rafael searched for the right person to help him with Apolonia.

Mallory tried to put herself in the younger girl's shoes, but couldn't. If her mother had died, it would have been unthinkable to have some stranger move into the Ellis house at Huntington Beach with Mallory and her father, no matter what sterling qualifications the woman possessed.

How cruel that Maria had to die.

It was even crueler that Apolonia's near drowning prevented her from visiting Maria yesterday. Neither of them had been able to say goodbye.

Heartsick, she wandered over to Apolonia's bed and looked down at her. She still wore her hair in a braid. It needed to be redone. The girl bore traits of both parents. One day she would be a beautiful woman in her own right.

Damn those boys who'd hurt Apolonia's feelings.

Mallory glanced at her watch. It was hard to see the dial through the blur. Yesterday at this time she and Lianor had just arrived at the hospital to visit Apolonia. Mallory had been so frightened she would discover the girl had developed complications. Yet miraculously the opposite had occurred and now she was home safe.

The sound of the door opening caused her to turn around.

''Rafael—'' she whispered. For no good reason her heart began to thud.

He'd emerged from his bedroom wearing causal trousers and a sport shirt in a cream tone, the perfect foil for his darkly handsome features and coloring. Those searching black eyes started at her bare feet and assessed her before she could finish wiping the moisture off her face.

''Is there something wrong?'' he whispered back, his expression solemn.

She took a few steps toward him. ''No. I was thinking about the timing of Maria's death.''

Rafael had to have been reading her mind because he said, ''Even if the accident hadn't happened, Maria was too far gone to talk to my daughter. I think it's better Apolonia's last memory of her was here at the palacio.''

''I'm sure you're right.'' She dashed away the last of her tears with her hand.

''How long has she been asleep?''

''About an hour and a half.''

"That means she'll be waking soon. Let's go to my suite until she does. I'll leave the door open."

After certain images that had filled her mind, it was strange to actually enter his bedroom which had been modernized like Apolonia's.

He led her past the king-size bed with its green and blue striped spread to his private balcony where a clear blue sky heralded another beautiful day. Far below them she could hear the occasional voice of someone enjoying the surf.

After seating her at the umbrella table where a veritable feast had been prepared, he found a chair opposite her and sat down. She knew it was an accident that his hand brushed her shoulder, but it electrified her body.

"I thought we would eat lunch out here. My sister is changing her clothes and will be with us any minute."

By the time he'd poured wine into their glasses, Lianor had appeared and took her place at the table. She looked drawn and upset. Except for a brief smile at Mallory, she didn't

say anything. Mallory had the feeling the two
of them had been arguing again.

"Try the prawns first," he said as if nothing
in the world was wrong. "They're marinated
in a special lime sauce I think you'll like."

Mallory was sure she would love them, just
as she loved everything about Portugal so far.

"Umm. They're fantastic!" she exclaimed
after eating one. "I could make a whole meal
of them."

"If you do that you'll hurt the chef's feelings. He prepared some of the palacio's most
famous dishes for you and hopes you'll taste
everything. People come from all over Europe
to eat his caldo verde, isn't that so, Lianor."

"Yes," she murmured. "It's a special rec-
ipe he makes with sausage, cabbage, potatoes
and olive oil."

"Let me give you some." Rafael ladled the
unusual-looking green soup into a bowl and
placed it in front of her.

She raised dazed eyes to his. "He shouldn't
have gone to all this trouble."

Rafael's black gaze gleamed between sooty
black lashes. The man was breathtaking.

"Felipe wanted to. He and Apolonia are great friends. What you did out there yesterday has won his loyalty along with the entire staff's."

To Mallory's consternation, she blushed. "Then I'll have to thank him personally."

"He'd like that."

The soup was unusual and superb. So was the sweet Serpa cheese and paella mixed with Algarve clams, bacon and the most delightful herbs she'd ever tasted.

"More meals like this and I won't be able to get around without a hoist."

Rafael's eyes played over her, missing nothing. "I should think your heavy responsibilities to your company will always keep you too busy to worry about that."

The coup de grace, delivered with exquisite timing.

CHAPTER FIVE

"MALLORY?" a young voice called urgently from the other room, breaking in on their frozen tableau.

"I'm right here, darling!" She started to get up but Rafael put a firm hand on her arm, preventing her from moving. Lines marred his face as they had earlier.

"You've done more than I could ever repay. I'll see to her."

The second he disappeared Lianor said, "I'm sure you can tell Rafael and I have been quarreling."

Mallory lowered her head. "It's none of my business, Lianor. The situation is impossible."

"Not if I quit work and come back home to take care of her." The last came out on a half sob. "But I don't think I can bear it, Mallory. There are things you don't know. Things that have been too pain—"

"Mallory!" Apolonia cried with relief and flew around to her side to hug her. "When I woke up, I thought you'd gone—"

She hugged her back, aware of Rafael's intense regard. He seemed to have lost color, as if he were ill. "I would never do that. According to your father, Felipe prepared all these special treats for me. I'm going to have to eat a little bit of everything to make it worth his while. What's your favorite?"

Apolonia looked over the food. "I like prawns the best."

"So do I. Come and sit by me. There are still plenty left."

Rafael helped his daughter into the chair before taking his place for the second time.

Mallory fixed a plate for her.

"Papa? When is Maria's funeral going to be?"

He stared at his daughter for a few seconds before he said, "The day after tomorrow."

"In our chapel?"

It didn't come as any surprise to Mallory that the palacio had a private sanctuary.

"Yes, *querida.* Lianor and I made all the arrangements with the priest."

While they ate in a strange kind of silence, one of the waiters came out on the balcony with a dessert tray. He took away some of the empty platters and placed it on the table.

"I don't think I have room for dessert," Mallory murmured.

"But you have to eat a *barriga de freiras.* Felipe has won a prize for them."

"A prize— Which one is it?"

Apolonia pointed to a luscious-looking pastry.

"What do you call it in English?"

"A nun's belly," her father drawled.

Mallory's gaze darted to his. "That's terrible!" she said, fighting a losing battle with laughter.

Despite his grave countenance, his lips twitched. "The tart next to it is called, heaven's lard."

"What's lard?" Apolonia wanted to know, but Mallory could hardly talk she was chuckling so hard.

"It's like butter," Rafael explained.

"Except that it doesn't burn as easily. I use it to make pie crust for apple pie. That's my father's favorite."

Apolonia's brown eyes widened. "You cook?"

"Every other Sunday I invite my parents for dinner. On the other Sundays I go home and help my mom cook."

"So you travel during the week."

Rafael had made one too many assumptions.

"Actually I'm not the one who leaves the office. That's up to the heads of sales and marketing. The only reason I was in New York was because the owner asked me to go on television to promote our products."

"You were on television?" his daughter asked.

"Yes. It was one of those night talk shows. Before I flew back to Los Angeles, I decided to take a few days off to visit Lianor. The truth is, I didn't really have business with her."

She saw the shocked glance he gave his sister.

"I'm so glad you came!" Apolonia cried.

"So am I, darling."

"Papa? As soon as we finish dessert, Mallory's going to help me make a book about Maria."

Lianor leaned forward. "What do you mean?"

Without preamble Apolonia explained everything. "...and someday I'll be able to read it to my little girl or boy so they'll know what Maria was like."

Another silence ensued. Lianor's eyes had filled with tears. Mallory didn't need to look at Rafael to feel his gaze leveled on her. At this point he obviously didn't know what to make of the notorious Lady Windemere.

The more she thought about his description of her, the more it rankled.

What hell for him to have to be grateful to her for saving Apolonia's life when she didn't qualify as a real woman in his eyes.

"I have an idea, Apolonia. Why don't we let your father eat the desserts while we get busy in your bedroom. Felipe will never know."

Rafael protested. "Stay where you are and enjoy the rest of your day with Lianor." On the surface he sounded the congenial host, but there was steel behind his words.

He reached across the table to pat Apolonia's hand. "I'll help you with the book, *querida*. Mallory's idea is a wonderful one. I'm reminded of moments with your mother and Maria before you were even born. We'll put it all in there."

"Can't the three of us do it together?"

Once again Mallory was the source of conflict.

"No, *querida*. You heard Mallory. She only came here to see Lianor, and so far they haven't spent any time together.

"I've taken the rest of my week off to be with you. Tomorrow we'll drive to Sintra to see Maria's friend, Eugenia, and bring her back with us."

"But tomorrow's not the funeral—"

"I've asked her to stay with us for a while."

"No, Papa—" Apolonia slid out of her chair and stood up. Tears rolled down her cheeks. "I don't want Eugenia to take care of me. She's old and cross."

Mallory's gaze flew to Lianor's. Her friend was in so much pain she could feel its pall from across the table. This was a nightmare.

"Eugenia's only going to be with us as long as it takes to find someone you will like."

"Don't get *her*—" By now Apolonia was sobbing.

"The matter is settled."

"No, Rafael." Lianor got to her feet. "Eugenia's a fine person, but she doesn't have the temperament to be around children. Apolonia's right. I—I'll give up my job and come back home."

"Thank God," her brother whispered.

Lianor looked at Mallory with despairing eyes. "Shall I turn in my resignation to you and have you take it to Los Angeles?"

Mallory knew it would break Lianor's spirit to have to quit. A lot more than wanting to be manager of the boutique lay at the heart of her struggles.

She had an idea Lianor's former weight problem was linked to her ill-fated love affair. It had scarred her so badly, she still couldn't deal with the painful memories. Maybe one day Lianor would be able to confide in Mallory.

As for Rafael, it killed her to realize the kind of pain he was in trying to solve a desperate situation. Their whole family was in turmoil, especially Apolonia whose only mother figure was being buried in two days.

Mallory loved that child.

Saving her life had bonded them in a way she couldn't explain. All she knew was that she wanted the young girl's happiness more than anything. Maybe she could take a sabbatical from her work...six months or a year, to help Apolonia through the transition period until Rafael found a permanent replacement for Maria.

Apolonia's suggestion that Mallory could still work for Lady Windemere was a very practical suggestion.

If the truth be told, she had an overwhelming desire to help care for Rafael's wonderful daughter. *If he would let her...*

Unfortunately his comments had left an indelible wound on her heart.

What you want isn't possible, querida. Mallory's not the motherly type and never will be. She's married to her work. One day she'll own a conglomerate.

A lot of men had branded Mallory without knowing the first thing about her. But *she* knew there were other whiz kids knocking at Liz's door more qualified than Mallory to replace her.

Liz would have no complaints as long as Mallory stayed on in an advisory capacity and could fly to L.A. for meetings once in a while. She could take Apolonia with her if she had to.

Mallory had been toying with the idea for days and having made up her mind, she put her napkin on the table and turned to Rafael's sobbing daughter.

''Apolonia?'' She reached for her hand and drew her close. ''Would you tell your father the question you asked me when you came to my room early this morning?''

After a lot of sniffing and wiping of eyes she said, ''I asked Mallory to be my nanny.''

A shocked sound came from Lianor's corner.

"I've given it a lot of thought," Mallory went right on speaking, "and I've decided I'd like the job until you've found the right person to replace Maria. That's pending your approval of course."

Rafael's groaned imprecation was lost in Apolonia's clear cry of joy. While she hugged her around the neck, he pushed himself away from the table and stood up, presenting a rather forbidding countenance.

"Apolonia? Would you please go to your room while I talk to Mallory?"

"But, Papa—"

"I'll take her," Lianor offered, visibly shaken herself. "Come on." She pulled her niece away from Mallory. The two of them disappeared into Rafael's bedroom.

His chest rose and fell with the weight of his emotions. She could tell he was close to letting go of his fury. "What in the name of all that's holy prompted you to say what you did in front of my daughter?"

"She told me she already talked to you about it. But to answer your question, I love her. We had an affinity from the first moment we met.

"Being Apolonia's nanny until you've found someone who would be the right person for her would satisfy something inside of me nothing else could. Liz will let me take a leave of absence whether it be six months or a year."

An angry laugh escaped. "You're Wall Street's poster girl."

She shot to her feet. "Let's get something straight, shall we? I'm a woman who went to college and obtained a law degree. I work for a company and enjoy it, but it's not the be-all and end-all of my existence."

His expression remained implacable. "Nevertheless, trying to fill a mother's role for Apolonia isn't like running a company or a law firm, whether it be for six months or a lifetime. You have no training for it."

"Did *you* when you became a father?" she fired back.

His hands formed fists at his side. "Maria planned to be with me indefinitely."

"I realize that. Won't you let me help you through this difficult time?"

His features looked chiseled. "Apolonia isn't a blue chip company listed on the stock market. She's my flesh and blood, someone I won't allow to be abandoned because a month from now you're offered a chairmanship you can't refuse," he bit out. "She has to have stability."

Mallory stood her ground. "You think I don't understand that wanting to look after her means making a commitment to remain with her until you've found someone else?"

"You can't guarantee that," he said in an icy tone.

"Why not?" Her eyes spit blue sparks. "People do take sabbaticals, you know. According to the female members of your family, you picture me as a machine without feminine needs or feelings. So if you're going to throw the argument in my face that I might get married and forsake Apolonia, it simply won't work!"

He studied her through veiled eyes. "After saving her life, I don't question the fact that you share a unique bond with her. But in two days you don't suddenly decide to give up an illustrious career to take care of a ten-year-old child in another country."

"I never said anything about giving it up, only that I would love to help Apolonia while you find the right person to replace Maria. Do you have a bias against Americans too?" When he didn't answer she said, "I only planned to stay with the company until it got on its feet. Then I intended to find something else more fulfilling.

"If I want to take some time off to be with an adorable ten-year-old girl who crawled straight into my heart, why does that threaten you?"

His jaw hardened. "What's your real motive, Mallory?"

"I've been investing my money so don't think I'm after yours. And it's *not* what your male vanity is assuming," she drove the point home, watching him stiffen. "But I guess when you're used to women throwing themselves at you, even the notorious Lady Windemere is suspect.

"Well you can think again, Rafael— Like you, I prefer my single status. If you hire me, you won't find me lying in wait for you on your bed one dark lonely night in the hope of trapping you. Since you never married again, it's obvious you're a one-woman man.

"If and when I decide to get married, it will be to a man who lives in the present, whose heart is wide open and dying to love me." After a pause she said, "I'll be happy to put that in writing if it will make you feel better."

The tension between them generated enough electricity to create lightning out of thin air. She was surprised it wasn't sparking all around them.

"My daughter's my life."

"I know," Mallory whispered. "I saw it in your eyes before you climbed in the ambulance after her. But before I knew that, something else happened in the ocean and on the beach." She paused for breath. "Apolonia became a part of me, and I, of her.

"You want the underlying motive for what I'm prepared to do? The only one I can give you is that she matters to me. Enough to want to take time off to be around her and help give her that stability you want for her."

"You say that now—"

"Because I mean it," she averred. "I don't know how else to explain this connection I feel to her. She feels it too. I realize I could never perform to Maria's standards. Apolonia and I would have to learn as we go. But it will be that way with anyone else you end up hiring."

She thought she might be getting through to him until he shook his dark head. "It won't work."

"Because of how it will look to other people?"

He skimmed the edge of his lower lip with his thumb. "Even if this were a match made in heaven, I have a reputation to uphold. There has been enough scandal in the past. I'll do anything to protect Apolonia."

Mallory had a gut feeling it involved Lianor.

"Then I guess that leaves you with no choice but to hire someone like Eugenia until you can find yourself a wife in a big hurry."

His black eyes flashed. "You know damn well I can't, not after you told my daughter you would take Maria's place. Do you honestly think she'll want anyone else now?"

"You're still her father," she reminded him. "I'll leave Portugal while you're holding the funeral services. Though Apolonia might be upset for a few days after I've gone, she'll accept whatever you think is best because she loves you. It won't be long before it's all forgotten."

She paused at the doorway to the balcony. "If you'll excuse me, I'm going to sunbathe on the beach while you spend the rest of the day with her."

Without waiting for a response, Mallory fled from his suite through the door to the corridor and flew down the staircase. Within a few minutes she'd reached her room at the other end of the palacio.

After throwing her clothes and toiletries in her suitcase, she grabbed the stationery out of the desk drawer and wrote a note to Felipe for the delicious meal, and a letter addressed to all three D'Afonsos.

Hoping Rafael would forgive her for her lie about leaving during the funeral, she propped it and the note on the dresser where Lianor would find them. Then she took another look around the suite to see if she'd forgotten anything.

Satisfied she'd packed everything, she rushed out of the palacio via the staircase next to the Alfama suite. On the outside steps she waited until she saw a taxi pulling up to the entrance.

Not daring to waste a second in case she was discovered, she ran the length of the palacio to catch up. As two people got out, she climbed in the back seat and told the driver to take her to the airport.

Forty-five minutes later she rushed inside the terminal to the ticket counter. To her dismay there were no flights to New York until morning, but she could board a flight to

London leaving straightaway. From there she'd be able to connect to an all-night flight leaving for Chicago.

Mallory paid for a ticket to England with her credit card and ran toward the gate to board the flight. She didn't expel the breath she'd been holding until the jet engines fired and she felt liftoff.

By the time the plane reached cruising speed, the tears she'd tried to prevent slid down her cheeks. She was no longer the same woman who'd flown to Portugal to visit Lianor on impulse. If anyone had told Mallory her life would be dramatically changed for the experience, she wouldn't have believed them.

Nevertheless, she was living proof that the impossible had happened.

It had only taken three days for her to realize she'd fallen painfully in love with Rafael and his daughter.

Since he'd refused to entertain the idea of her helping Apolonia through the transition, Mallory had been left with no choice but to bow out of their lives before his daughter grew any more attached to her.

But it hurt…

It hurt so much she wanted to die…

Still in a state of shock long after Mallory had disappeared, Rafael stood at the edge of the balcony looking out at the ocean. Much as he dreaded the inevitable confrontation with his daughter who was waiting for him in her bedroom, he feared something else kept him planted to the spot.

Through narrowed eyes he watched the activity on the beach. His heart hammered while he waited for Mallory's breathtaking body to enter his line of vision. But he waited in vain. Ten minutes passed before he decided she'd decided to sun herself on her private balcony.

Rafael had never lusted after a woman in his life. But if he remained out here any longer fantasizing about a moonlight swim with her, imagining her dark hair floating around them while they clun—

"Rafael?" The sound of Lianor's voice broke in on his intimate thoughts. "Apolonia wants to know how long you're going to be."

He took a shuddering breath before turning around. ''I'm coming.''

''Did Mallory really mean what she said?'' Her voice sounded unsteady. It appeared their visitor's offer to take Maria's place had thrown his sister almost as much as it had him.

''No. She was carried away by the moment.''

There was a prolonged silence. ''Where is she now?''

''She said something about taking a sunbathe.''

Lianor's expression grew haunted. ''Apolonia believes the two of you have been working things out.''

His jaw hardened. ''Everything's been arranged. Mallory's going to leave for the States during the funeral. When Apolonia discovers she's gone, I'm counting on *you* to be there for her. You did say you would quit your job and come home. Or were you carried away by the moment too?''

''No,'' Lianor said in a broken voice. ''Under the circumstances, I think Mallory better leave for California in the morning. I'll drive her to the airport early, before Apolonia can go looking for her.''

That's what was needed. A cold, clean separation. Something *final*.

Rafael knew it would be best for his daughter, yet the word 'final' gnawed away at his gut, propelling him toward Apolonia's bedroom. He found her at her desk with paper and pen in hand, intent on her thoughts. "How's it going?"

"I've written three pages." She glanced at him. "Where's Mallory?"

"She didn't want to intrude. Right now I believe she's resting." It wouldn't do to tell his daughter the truth. Otherwise she'd want to join their guest.

Apolonia put her pen on the top of the desk and stood up. "Are you going to let her take care of me?"

Stifling a groan, he hunkered down in front of her. "No, *querida.*"

Her eyes grew cold. He didn't know she could look like that. It sent a stabbing pain to his heart.

"You hate her don't you."

If only he did, he wouldn't be in this emotional turmoil right now.

"Not at all. I'm sure she would make a fine companion for you, but there are many reasons why I can't allow it."

"Not *her* reasons!" she fired back, shocking him. "Mallory said she wanted to take care of me. She wouldn't lie."

His daughter's faith in Mallory astounded him. "It's not that." He put his hands on her arms. "We can't have someone like her living with us the way Maria did."

"Why?" Her tear-filled eyes searched his.

"Because people would talk."

"About what?"

"Maria was a grandmother type. Mallory… isn't," his voice faded while his face grew hot just thinking about her.

"You mean she's a girlfriend type?"

He cleared his throat. "Something like that, yes."

"Vaz asked me if she was your girlfriend. I told him no. He said he was going to take her dancing."

Rafael's eyes closed for a moment. "You see the problem, *querida?* Even Vaz got an idea that wasn't true."

"I don't care."

"We have to care. There are a lot of unkind people who would think Mallory wasn't a nice woman to live in our home when she's not married. That wouldn't be fair to her."

"Maria wasn't married."

"That's different. She wasn't young enough to be my wife, so no one thought anything about it."

"Since you said you don't hate Mallory, you could marry her. Then everyone would think she was nice. Violente heard her father tell her mother that Mallory was even more beautiful than my mother. He said that if you let her go back to America, you are *insano*.

"And I heard Felipe tell the sous-chef that if he weren't married, he'd go after Mallory himself."

Por Deus. No man who got within sight of her was immune.

Unfortunately Apolonia couldn't help but be a walking encyclopedia of gossip, all of it to do with Mallory. The sooner she left Portugal, the better.

"*Querida*—you don't get married to someone unless you're both deeply in love."

"That's not true, Papa. You told Tia Lianor
that most women want to marry you for your
money. And on the phone the other day, I
heard you tell Antonio that Senhor Figuras
married his wife for her money."

Rafael smothered an epithet. He had no idea
his daughter had been listening to the conversation with his attorney.

"So why couldn't you marry Mallory so she
could be my nanny?"

Apolonia wasn't about to let this go. Her
clear, simple logic brought him to his feet.

"Let's not discuss Mallory right now. I
want to hear what you've written about Maria.
Then I'll fill in some parts."

"What if Mallory lived in an apartment in
Atalaia, and came to the palacio during the
day?" She'd ignored his suggestion by asking
another question. "Then would you let her be
my nanny?"

"No," he said with a note of finality.
"You're asking the impossible."

Her brown eyes which had been imploring, turned desolate like Lianor's when she was in pain.

"I—I wish Mallory hadn't saved me," she whispered before disappearing through their connecting door.

"Apolonia—"

Horrified, Rafael raced after her. By the time he caught up to her, she'd already left his bedroom and had reached their private stairway. Lianor was on her way up. The agonized look on her face checked their movements.

"What's wrong?" he demanded.

"Mallory's gone."

He felt as if a giant wave had slammed him against the rocks further up the coast, forcing the air out of his lungs.

"No—" Apolonia wailed before she broke down sobbing hysterically.

Rafael rushed toward his daughter, but Lianor reached her first and put an arm around her.

"She left a note for Felipe and a letter for us. Come on and sit down with me. I'll read it to you."

Reeling from the blow, he stood on the step behind them to listen.

"Dear Lianor, by the time you read this, I'll be on my way back to Los Angeles. Liz will understand why you had to resign, and she'll put one of the other saleswomen in charge of the shop until further notice. I consider you one of my dearest friends and will never forget you.

"I left today because your family needs privacy to mourn Maria's death, but I'm taking every beautiful memory of Portugal back with me.

"Apolonia? You will always live in my heart. I hope to meet you again one day when you're grown up and doing something exciting with your life and that wonderful, intelligent brain of yours. I'll miss you.

"Rafael? My thanks to you for your generous hospitality. The thrill of staying in a suite that belonged to a king will never leave me. Neither will my admiration for the way you've raised your daughter. She's delightful and very precious to me.

"May God keep the D'Afonso family in the safety of His arms.

Mallory."

While he was digesting the last of her letter, Apolonia broke free of Lianor's hold and ran down the rest of the stairs.

Lianor put her hand on his arm before he could tear after her. "Let her be alone for a few minutes."

"I can't," his voice shook. "Not after she just told me she'd rather be dead."

"Oh no—"

His daughter was in a precarious emotional state right now. Between losing Maria and recovering from a near drowning, he feared the news about Mallory would land her back in the hospital.

To his surprise he found Apolonia in his study. She'd perched herself on the edge of his chair and was typing something on the keyboard of his computer. Every few seconds he heard her sobs.

Maybe it would be wise to let her play some games until she'd calmed down enough to be rational. But when he reached her side, he realized she'd gone online. After a series of clicks, a cartoon image of an Amazon woman from a comic book appeared on the screen.

Apolonia pressed the print button and out it came. An eight and a half by eleven inch of a female who bore a superficial resemblance to Mallory.

She took it out of the printer, then stared at him with angry eyes. "I hate you, Papa," she blurted before trying to slip away. Rafael caught hold of her and forced a hug.

"You don't mean that," he whispered against her wet cheek.

"Yes I do. Because of you she went away and I'll never see her again. I didn't even get to say goodbye."

The tremor in her voice, the heaving of her body defeated him.

"I have an idea." He cradled the back of her head where he could feel the braid Mallory had fixed for her. "After the funeral, how would you like to take a trip with me? Anywhere you want to go."

He heard a slight gasp before she lifted her tear-ravaged face. "Can we go to Disneyland?"

What she'd really asked was, could they go see Mallory? The hope in her eyes staggered him.

"Is that the only place you can think of?"

"No, but my friend Garbriela went with her family and she loved all the rides. Mallory said you would get scared on the Matterhorn."

His daughter had a one-track mind. "When did she tell you this?"

"This morning while we were looking at pictures on the Internet. I'll show you!"

Animated once more, she broke away long enough to sit at the computer. He watched her deft movements as she clicked on the history button. Up came a picture of a frog.

"See? This is Mr. Toad. She said there's a wild ride named after him." Without pausing for breath she told Rafael the story of the *Wind in the Willows.*

"What else did she show you?" Mallory had a way of doing the unexpected, ensnaring him no matter how he fought against it.

''There's a picture of the man she plans to marry when he's available.''

An explosion went off inside his taut frame. Mallory had *lied* to him.

''Do you want to see him?''

''Not particularly,'' he muttered. With one touch of the button, he shut off the computer. ''I was thinking of taking you for a drive. Maybe Violente would like to come with us.''

His daughter slid off the chair and walked at his side. ''I can't wait to show her the man Mallory loves. He's got blond hair and it's curly. There aren't any men in Portugal who look like him!''

Rafael's teeth ground together. No doubt her dream man was some prominent, high-profile Wall Street tycoon waiting in the wings for her.

''She says she would marry him right this second if she could because he makes her heart beat fast. His name—''

''Let's talk about the trip, shall we? It will probably be hot in Los Angeles. You won't need to take anything but some pants and light-weight tops.''

CHAPTER SIX

THE Friday morning board of directors meeting for Lady Windemere was halfway through when Mallory's secretary buzzed her.

She picked up the phone. "Yes, Barb?"

"I've got Sue from reception on the line."

"Yes, Sue?"

"Sorry to interrupt, but you've got visitors."

"They'll have to make an appointment with Barb."

"No, no. You don't understand," she said in hushed tones. "There's this fantastic, and I mean *fantastic*-looking man in the foyer who could have stepped out of a painting in the Prado.

"He speaks in this deep sexy voice with an accent, and he's got a cute little girl with him. But he refused to give me his name. Apparently his daughter wanted to surprise you."

Mallory's heart rolled over and over until she could hardly breathe.

Rafael—

He was actually here in L.A. with Apolonia? In the building?

"I—I'll be right out," she stammered like a schoolgirl.

With a trembling hand she hung up the phone. Her gaze shot to Liz. "Something's come up I have to see about. Please go on with the meeting."

The owner eyed her with a curious glance before nodding. She knew about the situation in Lisbon and Mallory's thwarted desire to take care of Apolonia for a temporary period. But Liz had been waiting to talk to Lianor about her resignation until Monday. With the D'Afonso family still grieving, she felt it would be better to hold off. So did Mallory.

After her last confrontation with Rafael, she never expected to see him again. She could understand his wanting to take Apolonia on a trip. Anything to get her mind off Maria for a little while until she could cope with her loss. But to come to California and seek out Mallory at her office made no sense if he didn't want more problems.

It was too soon to see him again.

She'd been an emotional wreck since her return. No appetite, no sleep for the last few nights. Before the meeting Liz had remarked on how pale she looked this morning.

The peach top and pants she was wearing had washed her out even more. However Mallory hadn't been thinking about the way she looked after surviving another wretched night. In truth she couldn't seem to focus on anything, not even the legal affairs of the company.

She didn't *want* to focus on them.

The trip to Lisbon had changed her so completely, she didn't know herself anymore. Last night she'd poured out her heart to her parents. They'd listened and commiserated, but for the first time in her life she didn't feel any better after unburdening herself to them.

Mallory wasn't sure she could handle seeing Rafael a second time no matter how brief their meeting might be. If Apolonia weren't with him, she would refuse.

Liar, said a little voice as she hurried down the hall toward reception with her heart beating faster than a hummingbird's.

"Mallory!"

Apolonia ran across the room and threw her arms around her waist. While Mallory hugged her back, she lifted her eyes to Rafael.

Sue had spoken the truth. He did look fantastic. In fact there were no adjectives in English or any other language that could describe a man whose Mediterranean blood set him apart from other men.

She'd never seen him in jeans before. They molded to his powerful thighs while the pale blue knit shirt covered the top half of his physique like a second skin. It revealed the definition of toned muscle in his arms and chest most males would kill to possess.

"*Bom dia,* Mallory." His voice grated. "We arrived from Lisbon last night and checked into the Disneyland Hotel."

Beneath a head of wavy black hair and dark brows she met his gaze head-on. In those fiery black depths she could read accusation.

Why?

Was he upset because she'd left without saying goodbye? She'd done it with the best of intentions.

"I see." She tried to swallow but her mouth had gone dry. "I—Is Lianor with you?"

"No. Until we return, she's training one of the saleswomen at the boutique to take over until a new manager is appointed. Have you told the owner she has resigned?"

Nothing had changed. He was adamant his sister move back home and help him raise his daughter. Mallory's spirits took a nosedive.

"Yes. I was just in a meeting with Liz. She said she planned to contact Lianor on Monday."

"Good," he muttered with obvious relief. "Then it's settled. I told Apolonia we'd take a short trip after Maria's funeral. She has always wanted to come to Disneyland."

"I'm glad you got home safe," his daughter interjected.

"I warned her you'd be at work and too busy to do anything more than say hello."

So that was what all this was about? A trip to appease Apolonia in her bereavement? A

token stop at Mallory's work because his
daughter hadn't been able to say goodbye to
her earlier in the week?

Mallory was no fool. She could read between the lines. She'd heard the cleverly dis-
guised demand in his tone. Rafael expected her
to back him up and would be furious if she
didn't.

Well she had news for him!

With a deliberate smile she said, "I'm as
free as the wind." Then her gaze dropped to
his daughter. "Let me grab my purse and some
passes for us. We'll explore Disneyland from
one end to the other."

Apolonia beamed. "It's so big! Won't it
take more than one day?"

"With the summer crowds I'm sure of it."

An anxious look entered her brown eyes.
"Will you be able to come with us tomorrow
too?"

"I'm planning on being your guide for as
long as you're in California," Mallory declared. "As of this minute, I'm on vacation
with you. On Sunday we'll eat dinner at my
parents' home in Huntington Beach. They've

heard all about you and are anxious to meet you.''

Again she felt the younger girl burrow against her with happiness. Mallory lifted her head to stare straight at Apolonia's father. *Think on that, Rafael D'Afonso.*

''By the way, how long did you say you were staying in California before *you* have to get back to work Rafael?''

He folded his arms across his broad chest. No doubt he was having difficulty controlling his emotions now that she'd sabotaged his plans.

''We're flying home on Monday. I have business I can't put off any longer.''

''Then we'd better get in as much fun as we can.''

''I love you, Mallory.''

''Ditto.''

''What does that mean?''

''It means, I love you too.'' Her gaze flicked back to Rafael's. ''I assume you're driving a rental car.''

A forbidding frown had settled into place. Once again they faced each other as adversaries. He gave an almost imperceptible nod.

"Why don't you follow me to my apartment while I pack an overnight bag? That way I can stay at the hotel with you."

His firm jaw hardened into rock at that piece of news. He was angry, but that was just too bad.

She fastened her attention on Apolonia. "On the way to Disneyland we'll stop at Knott's Berry Farm and visit Camp Snoopy. He's this cute little dog in a cartoon everyone adores.

"We'll grab a bite of lunch there on a patio by the Grizzly Creek Falls. You'll love it. You can send Violente some postcards and she'll be *soooo* envious."

Apolonia squealed in delight.

"In fact you can buy her a Snoopy for a gift to take home. She'll treasure it. Now—give me a minute to let my secretary know I won't be back until further notice. Then I'm all yours."

Leaving that assertion floating in the same air Rafael breathed, she hurried past Sue who was all eyes and ears. By the time she reached her office, excitement had such a tight hold on her Barb chuckled.

Ignoring her reaction she said, ''I need three Disneyland passes.''

Her secretary pulled them from the file cabinet and handed them to her. ''I thought these were for Lady Windemere families only.''

''I won't tell if you won't,'' she said, wishing the three of them were a family in the legal sense of the word.

''And here we all thought your business trip to Portugal had been uneventful. Good grief—the man's incredible! Every woman in the building is dying over him.''

Hot-faced, Mallory murmured, ''It's his daughter I'm crazy about.''

''Whatever you say.''

''I'm taking today and Monday off. Will you tell Liz for me?''

''Of course.''

''She can always reach me on my cell phone.''

"Go. Get out of here. We'll hold down the fort while you're having the time of your life with Mr. Scrumptious."

Since Barb's assumption was patently true, there was no point in denying it.

Mallory had left Portugal without warning because she'd felt it was best for Apolonia. Now everything had changed. Rafael had brought his daughter all the way across an ocean and a continent to her office. As far as she was concerned she was at war, with Apolonia and her father the prize.

Mallory's first tactical maneuver was to become the girl's nanny. Then she'd go after the rest of the spoils by fair means or foul.

As the creator of the Amazon women cartoon series had once said, *"Women are the nature-endowed soldiers of Aphrodite, goddess of love and beauty, and theirs is the only conquering army to which men will permanently submit—not only without resentment or resistance or secret desires for revenge, but also with positive willingness and joy!"*

After retrieving her purse from the bottom desk drawer in her office, she put the passes inside and headed for the entrance to the building. *Ooh* how she relished the thought of their next skirmish. In fact her adrenaline was surging.

When she caught up to her visitors, Rafael was in deep conversation with his daughter about something. She could guess he was reminding her this was only a trip. On Monday they would have to say a final goodbye.

Over my dead body.

He cut it off when he saw Mallory and straightened to his full height.

She flashed him an ingenuous smile. "My car is parked at the side of the building. It's a red Toyota. Come on, Apolonia." She reached for the girl's hand. "I only live five minutes from here. You can drive with me and tell me about the funeral."

Rafael followed them out the double doors into the sun. It was a nice day for L.A. Not too hot yet. Very little smog for a change. They walked the length of the building lined with palm trees.

"I asked Papa to buy white roses like you said. When I put them on her grave, I took one out and kept it for my book."

"Have you finished it?"

"Yes. I brought it with me. Do you want to see?"

"I can't wait to read it and look at the pictures. We'll do it tonight before we go to bed." Which reminded her she needed to make a hotel reservation on the way to her condo.

They rounded the corner and headed for her car.

"When we get to Disneyland, can we go on Mr. Toad's Wild Ride first?"

"Of course. It's in Fantasyland, my favorite place." She used her remote to unlock the doors and they got in. Rafael approached her side of the car while the two of them buckled up. He wore an inscrutable expression. Apolonia's father was not a happy camper.

"I'm driving a white Buick two rows away."

"We'll wait for you. Don't worry about getting lost. We don't have to drive on the freeway. But just in case, here's my cell phone number.'' She wrote it down on the back of one of her business cards and handed it to him.

She sensed his hesitation before he strode off in the direction of his rental car. No doubt he was muttering something too indelicate for feminine ears. Even so, Mallory couldn't take her eyes off him.

Reaching for her purse, she pulled out a pass to get a phone number off it. When she'd made the connection and waited for reservations to answer, she found her credit card.

''What floor are you on at the hotel, Apolonia?''

''Number five.''

By now Rafael had pulled behind them. It sent delicious chills through her body to know he was so close instead of being thousands of miles away in his palacio.

After a bit of haggling with the reservationist, she was able to get a room on the fourth floor. She gave her credit card number and the deed was done.

''Let's go.''

She drove to the main street and merged with the traffic. Apolonia exclaimed about everything she saw. So many questions. Mallory loved answering every one of them.

It didn't take long to reach her condo three miles away. It was in a two-storied refurbished fifties building with eight units. She'd gotten it for a good price as far as housing in California was concerned.

Since earning a salary, she'd been making double payments on the mortgage, and invested the rest of her money. Thus she lived meagerly. In time her efforts would pay off.

Her unit was on the main floor at the back. She drove around to her stall and used her arm to signal the visitor parking for Rafael.

He'd exited his car and had caught up to them before she and Apolonia had reached the door to the complex. He took hold of his daughter's hand.

"We'll wait for you out here."

Mallory stiffened. "This may not be the Palacio D'Afonso, but it's my home here in Los Angeles. I'd like to return your hospitality if you'll let me."

With those words, whatever he'd been ready to say didn't come out. Taking that as an assent, she opened the door with her remote and they entered the building. She used her key to let them inside the first condo on her right.

The living room was the largest in her tiny one-bedroom domicile. It resembled a library with hundreds of books and magazines, the majority of them legal, economic and financial. They were stuffed into wicker shelving.

In a box on the floor next to one stand-up shelf lay her college degrees, awards, surfing trophies and junk she didn't know what to do with.

The room served as her office. Her computer sat on top of an old oak desk she'd found at a garage sale along with a love seat, chair and floor lamp. There was a picture on the wall of Mallory when she was seven, along with her parents and the family dog. That was it for the decorating. Nothing matched. Louvered blinds at the windows instead of curtains. The hardwood floors were its only saving grace.

One glimpse of Rafael's eyes taking everything in had to reinforce his opinion she was the ultimate corporate type without the feminine instincts most women possessed.

''While you make yourself comfortable, Apolonia and I will get us some drinks.'' The only thing she had on hand was diet raspberry. It would have to do.

His daughter followed her into the miniscule kitchen. Her curious brown eyes looked around in fascination.

''I told you I felt like a mouse at the palacio.''

That comment prompted Apolonia to laugh her charming laugh. Mallory took two large glasses from the cupboard and filled them partway with ice. She reached in the fridge for two cans of soda. After they were poured, she found some paper napkins.

Together they carried everything back to the living room. To her surprise Rafael had hunkered down to look through her box of stuff.

''Here you go.''

He rose to his feet and took the glass from her. When her fingers brushed against his warm flesh, a tingling sensation spread through her body.

''Thank you,'' he murmured in an oddly husky tone.

"While you relax, I'll change."

On her way out, she pulled a book about SeaWorld off the shelves and placed it next to Apolonia who sat on the couch. "If you can talk your father into staying a little longer, this is another place we ought to visit while you're here."

She disappeared down the hall to her bedroom smiling all the way.

Discarding her clothes, she put on designer jeans and a white crocheted top with cap sleeves. To keep the hair out of her face on the rides, she made a fat braid and layered it on her head, securing it with a tortoiseshell comb.

Liz had remarked on her pallor, but when Mallory looked in the bathroom mirror, her cheeks were flushed. She applied her favorite cherry-red lipstick, a touch of Lady Windemere's Wild Flower spray and she was ready.

Once she'd packed her toiletries in her overnight bag, she added two outfits, fresh underwear, a nightgown and her white robe, then closed it. As she left the bedroom, she snatched her camera from the dresser.

Her purse was in the kitchen. When she reached it, she slipped the camera inside and walked into the living room.

Rafael sat next to his daughter while he leafed through one of Mallory's law books.

"You look beautiful!" Apolonia cried. "I wish you would fix my hair like that."

Rafael's gaze clapped on her like a magnet. The book slid from his hands and plopped on the floor. He gathered it and put it back on the shelf.

"Do you want me to do it now?"

"Will you?"

"I'd be happy to. Let me get another clip from the bathroom."

In a few minutes the girl wore Mallory's identical hairdo. While she ran in the bathroom to get a glance in the mirror, Mallory took the cans and empty glasses back to the kitchen. When she re-entered the living room, Apolonia came running.

"Papa—Mallory and I are twins. How do I look?"

In jeans and a white top, Mallory thought they could almost pass for mother and daughter.

"You...both look lovely," came the quiet aside.

Mallory tried not to laugh at the way he'd hesitated before including her in the compliment.

"That's high praise coming from your father. Shall we go?"

He paused at the door. "I'll drive us from here on out."

That might be bad news if he decided to bring her back at the end of the day whether she had a hotel reservation or not. But she chose to risk it because she loved being taken care of by him. It felt like they were going on a real family outing.

The rest of the day passed in a blur of excitement. Apolonia was so ecstatic, it rubbed off on her father. Until it was time to say goodnight at the hotel, he'd gotten into the spirit of things like every father, enchanting Mallory to her very bones.

She couldn't wait to get her film developed. Rafael didn't know it but she'd snapped dozens of pictures of him laughing or smiling at the odd moment. These photos would be for her private delectation.

During their outing most women paused in their tracks to stare at him with unabashed interest. According to Apolonia, one eager female on the Pirates of the Caribbean had been bold enough to tell him she was staying at the same hotel. If he wanted to go out for cocktails later, she was in room 210.

That brought out a possessive streak in Mallory she didn't know she could feel. But what the other woman didn't realize was that Mallory had Apolonia on her side. She intended to use it to her advantage.

By the time Rafael escorted them to the door of her hotel room, they were pleasantly exhausted and overloaded with souvenirs. It was in this happy state that Mallory decided now would be the perfect time to follow through with the next stage in her plan. Her room had two queen-size beds.

She put her arm around Apolonia. "How would you like to stay with me tonight? You can read your book to me before we fall asleep. In the morning we'll order breakfast and your father can join us before we go on the rest of the rides."

"Could I, Papa? Please?"

To add the kicker Mallory said, "I heard you met a woman on one of the rides who's staying at this hotel. Apolonia and I don't care if you take her for drinks, do we?"

"No. You can stay out as late as you want, Papa. Mallory and I are going to have fun."

A grimace added lines to his handsome face. If he weren't a civilized man, Mallory figured she'd be dead by now.

She patted Apolonia's arm. "Why don't you go to your room with your father and talk things over. Ring me if you decide to stay with him tonight."

Without hesitation she moved inside her room and shut the door. Unashamed of what she'd done, she hurried into the shower to wash her hair and get ready for bed.

After ten minutes, still no phone call.

She used the blow-dryer, then slipped on her robe. No sooner had she tied the sash than she heard a rap on the door and hurried to open it.

"Come on in."

"I love that robe," was the first thing Apolonia declared upon entering. "Don't you think it's pretty, Papa?"

Mallory was already trembling because she thought she'd glimpsed a flash of desire in Rafael's black eyes during the first few seconds of seeing him in the entry. But on second glance they were veiled, causing her to wonder if she'd been mistaken because she wanted desperately to be desirable to him.

"Yes," came the begrudging utterance. He walked past her to put Apolonia's suitcase on one of the beds.

For ten years he hadn't found a woman he wanted to marry. However if Mallory had anything to say about it, his bachelorhood was about to come to an end. She wanted Rafael to realize how much he needed her.

She hugged Apolonia who was carrying her new plush animal Mr. Toad in one arm, and Snoopy in the other. "My mother could make you one in your size just like it. On Sunday we'll ask her.''

''I can't wait to see your house.''

''It would still only take up a little bit of space in your private residence at the palacio. Any mice who came to dinner at my parents' would feel as tall as the grown-ups.''

A smile lit up her eyes before she laughed, ''You're so fun, Mallory. I had the best time of my life today.''

''So did I, darling. Now, let's undo your braid and get you into the shower to wash your hair. Afterward you can take a Lady Windemere bubble bath.''

''What's that?''

Mallory flicked her glance to Rafael whose eyes had been playing over her. Did it mean he liked what he saw? ''Would you explain to your daughter?''

''Explain what?''

Her pulse rate bounced off the charts to realize he hadn't been paying attention to the conversation. Nothing could have excited her more. She went into the bathroom and brought out a bottle.

He looked at it and said something in Portuguese to his daughter.

Apolonia made an excited sound and took it from him. "Would you like to try it too before you go out tonight, Papa? I'll start my bath right now. Don't go away!" She disappeared behind the bathroom door.

Mallory heard a swift intake of breath. "Now that we have a moment to ourselves, there's something I have to say to you."

She folded her arms. "Go ahead."

His features had taken on a chiseled cast. "After the way you left Portugal, I thought you understood the precariousness of the situation."

"I do," she asserted.

"Then why in the hell did you exacerbate the problem this morning by making yourself available for the entire weekend? Apolonia's in heaven right now, but when we have to leave on Monday it's going to be another story."

"You should have thought of that before you brought her to my office," she stated in a level voice. ''When I'm around her I can't help it if my natural instincts come out.''

He eyed her forcefully. ''Tomorrow night when I drive you back to your condo, you'll come up with a convincing reason why we can't spend Sunday with you or have dinner at your parents' home. I don't care how big a lie it is as long as my daughter understands she can't manipulate either of us any longer.''

Mallory cocked her head to the side, causing her glossy dark-brown mane to settle over one shoulder like mist. ''She'll fall apart, Rafael.''

His compelling mouth became a white line of anger. ''Tell me something I don't already know.''

Unable to resist, she said, ''Enjoy your night out. Everything they say about California girls is true.''

Fire flared in those black eyes before he stormed out of her hotel room. She was surprised he still had enough control left not to slam the door in her face. If they'd been at the palacio, he would have shown no such restraint. Mallory could almost hear the sound reverberating up and down the great corridor.

But once he'd gone, she remembered his warning about tomorrow. A dark depression settled around her like a thick fog shrouding the beach.

No visibility. No hope of the sun coming out.

Over the next twenty-four hours Mallory had to pretend all was wonderful. In reality, every passing moment was bittersweet. Rafael seemed to enjoy the day, yet somehow avoided any eye contact with her. If he'd gone for drinks or anything else with that other woman, Mallory had no way of knowing.

Apolonia thrilled to everything of course, especially Tinkerbell's Magic Sound and Fireworks Show, the last event to top off another exciting day. Throughout the dazzling display Mallory hadn't been able to concentrate, not when she could hear the ticking of the time bomb which would explode once they reached her condo.

"Papa? Can we go to SeaWorld tomorrow?" Apolonia asked the question twenty minutes later. She sat up in the front seat of the car with her father.

From the back Mallory moaned in panic.

"Yes, *querida*. We'll stay in San Diego tomorrow night, and fly back home from there
on Monday."

"But we're going to Mallory's house for
dinner."

Here it comes.

"I'm afraid that's impossible. Do you want
to tell her, Mallory?"

She had to clear her throat several times.
"While you were getting your picture taken
with Mickey Mouse, my mother rang me on
my cell phone. My Uncle Steven is very sick,
and so my parents have to go see him tomorrow."

"Is he sick like Maria was?" Her voice
wobbled.

"He has a bad heart." It was the truth, but
he wasn't dying. Not yet. "They are so sorry
they won't be able to meet you this trip."

"Do you love your uncle?"

"Of course she does," Rafael interjected.
"Just the way you love Tia Lianor. That's why
Mallory's going to have to be with her parents

all day tomorrow, but we'll have a great time at SeaWorld anyway.''

For the rest of the drive home quiet sobs punctuated the silence. When Rafael found a space in the visitor parking, Apolonia undid her seat belt and turned around in the seat to look at Mallory.

''Can I stay with you tonight?''

''No.'' her father proclaimed in a tone of authority Mallory recognized was final.

She reached out to squeeze Apolonia's arm. ''I'll never forget these last two days.''

Fresh tears spurted from her eyes. ''I don't want to go to SeaWorld without you.''

''In that case we'll fly home tomorrow.'' On that definitive note Rafael levered himself from the front seat to retrieve Mallory's overnight bag in the trunk. Unable to bear it another second, she jumped out of the car.

So did Apolonia. She grabbed on to Mallory's hand with all her might. ''Do you think you could come to the palacio on another vacation next week?''

Her father put the overnight bag down and picked her up. ''It's not polite to ask so many questions.''

''But I don't want to leave Mallory,'' she cried hysterically. It caught the attention of Bob Sargent, an attractive blond script writer who'd just gotten out of his car and lived in the condo across the hall from her.

He darted Mallory a quick smile which for no apparent reason seemed to enflame Rafael even more.

''*Adeus,* Mallory,'' his voice grated. ''Thank you for showing us a wonderful time at Disneyland. We won't forget.''

''No Papa—'' Apolonia's screams were so loud, he picked her up and carried her to his car. ''Mallory loves me and I love her. If you make Tia Lianor take care of me, I'll run away,'' Mallory heard her tell her father. Apolonia's emotions were out of control.

It was a nightmarish scene, but Rafael was only trying to save his daughter from worse heartbreak down the line.

Mallory knew exactly how Apolonia felt because she was experiencing the same debilitating sense of loss.

Wild with pain, she picked up her suitcase and hurried inside the condo to block out the girl's cries. But even after she'd shut the door, they resounded in her heart. The poor darling had lost Maria. Now all that pain was coming out.

After five minutes Mallory realized she couldn't stay at her condo tonight. She needed someone to talk to before she went mad.

Without wasting a moment, she ran in her bedroom and repacked her overnight case with clean clothes. Once she'd gotten in her car and had made her way to the freeway, she would phone her parents and let them know she was coming.

She'd almost reached the door of her condo when her cell phone rang. At twelve-thirty at night it had to be her mom wanting to make final arrangements for Sunday dinner. Under the circumstances her timing couldn't have been more welcome.

Putting down her suitcase, she undid her purse to get it.

"Mom?"

"No," sounded a deep male voice. "It's Rafael."

Mallory felt so faint she had to take refuge in her only chair. "Wh-Where are you?"

"Outside your condo."

They hadn't left yet?

"We need to talk."

She closed her eyes. *Agreed.* Her heart was galloping loud enough for him to hear it.

"Why don't you bring Apolonia inside. I know she's exhausted. We can put her down on my bed so she'll sleep."

"We'll be right in."

One minute later a pale, subdued Apolonia entered the building with her father. She wrapped her arms around Mallory's waist without saying anything.

"Come on in and lie down, darling." She guided her through the condo to the bedroom. "Up you go." She helped lift her, then took off her sandals. "Dream about Sleeping Beauty's Castle," she said after covering her with the quilt. "Your father and I will be in the other room if you want us."

"I love you," the girl whispered. Her eyelids fluttered closed.

After giving her a kiss on the forehead, Mallory turned off the light and joined Rafael. He stood in the middle of the room with his hands on his hips in that striking male stance he wasn't aware of. The shadowy light revealed his anguish.

Their gazes fused.

"I brought Apolonia to California for one reason only. To test your sincerity about wanting to be her nanny."

"And I failed it?" Mallory demanded.

His features hardened. "You know damn well you didn't. Can you tell me now, this instant, that you're prepared to take care of my daughter as if she were your own until I find someone else?"

It was happening.

"I am."

In fact I've given it a lot of thought and would like to be Maria's permanent replacement. It's all I've been able to think about.

"Even if it means marrying me?" he ground out.

CHAPTER SEVEN

AT THAT question Mallory could hardly breathe for the joy spreading through her system. But she had to be careful not to let it show.

"We don't have to go that far do we?" she answered in a smooth tone. "I've put up with gossip all of my adult life. It won't bother me."

"Perhaps not," he bit out. "However where I come from, a single woman who looks like you, living in a single man's household like mine, isn't acceptable in polite society. I'm raising Apolonia to be a lady like her mother."

She crossed her fingers behind her back. "As long as Apolonia knows you and I won't be living as man and wife in private, it's fine with me either way."

"Marriage was my daughter's suggestion to this untenable situation."

Mallory felt the point of that fiery dart penetrate her soul. But it meant Apolonia had found a way around her father's objections. That salient truth flooded Mallory with happiness.

She shrugged her shoulders. "If *you're* willing, I guess there's no problem as long as your girlfriends understand that's all they can be to you until you're legally free of me."

His expression looked like thunder.

This was getting fun.

"Since I'm an attorney, I can draw up a prenuptial agreement with your attorney. We'll word it so it prevents me from taking anything but a salary from you over the next eight years, and nothing after our divorce but my clothes and suitcase. Fair enough?"

At this point his eyes were mere slits. "Apolonia told me you're in love with someone and would marry him immediately if he were available."

"But he isn't," Mallory played along. Had his daughter purposely left out the fact that it was Flash Gordon? If she was intelligent and clever enough to suggest marriage in order to find a way to have Mallory for her nanny, she was capable of teasing him for her own purposes. She was Rafael's daughter after all.

''He might never become available. Suffice it to say, Apolonia will be my only priority. I'll add that to the prenuptial agreement so there can be no question of my abandoning her.''

''You'll have to pretend to be my wife in public and live in my suite so the staff doesn't talk.''

''Naturally. Otherwise there'd be no point to this elaborate charade. With Apolonia's bedroom right next to yours, I can slip through the connecting door every night and sleep in the extra bed. Besides I understand you travel quite often.

''Unlike a wife, I won't ask questions about the women you're with when you're away from the palacio. I plan to live my own life taking care of your daughter. I intend to let you live yours.''

Rafael tossed his head back. The man had been caught in a snare of his daughter's making and he didn't like it one bit. *But he would...*

"When do you want our wedding to take place?"

"As soon as possible," he said in a clipped tone. "The priest will marry us in the family chapel."

Another dream was coming true.

"I'll ask mom and dad to come over in the morning. They can bring her wedding dress for me to pack. We're the same height and build. She made it herself and has been saving it for me."

At that bit of unsolicited information he raked a hand through his black hair. It was a sure sign he'd started to feel the tightening of her golden lasso and it was making him nervous.

"What will you do with your condo?"

"Sublet it. When you've found someone else for Apolonia, I'll leave Portugal and come back here to live. My parents will help me move the things I want stored to their house. Mom's been needing a new car. She can use mine until I need it again."

Mallory could tell she was moving way too fast for him, but she wasn't about to let him back out of their deal now.

''I can be ready to fly to Lisbon with you on Monday. If you'll tell me your flight information, I'll make a reservation.''

She heard him expel his breath as if the weight of the world were on his shoulders. ''I'll take care of it.''

For a man who'd been living a bachelor life for the last ten years, the thought of a temporary wife, even one in name only, must sound like the worst penance imaginable.

His eyes impaled her. ''What about your job?''

Ah yes. The one she was married to.

''Liz already knows I would like to be Apolonia's nanny. The night your daughter broached the subject, I spent a good hour on the phone with her from the palacio discussing how we would work things out if you decided to hire me for an interim period.''

His body went taut. Something she'd just said had hit him wrong again.

"You look tired, Rafael. Why don't you go back to the hotel and get a good sleep. In the morning you can come for Apolonia and tell her what's been decided."

"Papa?"

They both turned around in surprise to see Apolonia standing there in her bare feet. She ran over to him. "Are you really going to marry Mallory?" she cried.

Mallory had often heard the expression 'stars in her eyes,' but until now she'd never witnessed such a phenomenon.

He hunkered down. "Yes, *querida*."

"Oh Papa. I'm so happy!" She threw her arms around his neck.

Tears welled in Mallory's eyes despite all efforts to hold them back.

"If you're happy, that's all that matters," he whispered, but Mallory heard him.

One day Rafael would be totally happy too. She planned to take care of it personally.

"Can we stay here tonight?"

He shook his head. "Mallory only has one bed, but we'll come back tomorrow to help her move."

Yes, yes, yes!

Apolonia pulled away from him to hug Mallory.

Rafael's inscrutable gaze met hers. "We'll be by at eight-thirty with breakfast."

"That will be perfect."

She walked them to the door, watching and listening to Apolonia who talked excitedly to her taciturn father all the way out of the building.

Mallory couldn't wait until her parents met her future daughter and husband tomorrow! Then they'd understand everything. But there was one person who needed to hear the news from Mallory right now.

She reached for her purse to pull out her cell phone and little address book. It was Sunday morning in Lisbon. Hopefully Rafael's sister was awake.

After three rings she heard a click. *"Alo?"*

"Bom dia, Lianor." There was no time like the present to start speaking Portuguese. One day Mallory intended to be fluent in the language.

"Mallory?" The other woman sounded shocked.

"Yes. Did you get my letter to your family?"

"Of course, and I gave Felipe your note. He was very touched. Mallory—" There was a long pause. "I—I've been waiting to hear from Liz, but she still hasn't phoned me. What's going on?"

"That's why I'm calling." Mallory subsided into the chair. "Rafael brought Apolonia to my office yesterday morning."

A longer silence ensued this time. Then she heard, "Apolonia was heartbroken when you left Portugal without telling her. I'm not surprised my brother let her come to say a proper goodbye to you."

"Actually, we didn't say goodbye. In fact we've been together ever since." Mallory launched into an explanation of their activities. "Just a few minutes ago he asked me to marry him so I could be Apolonia's nanny without raising any eyebrows. I accepted his proposal because I love her and want to take care of her."

She heard a quiet gasp coming from the other end of the phone.

"Don't worry, Lianor. Ours will be a true marriage of convenience, but it's worth it to ensure Apolonia's happiness...and yours," Mallory added. "That's why you've never received a phone call from Liz. You can go on managing the shop."

"You're in love with my brother aren't you," she came back at last.

"Yes," Mallory whispered. "But it will have to be our secret. Do you mind that we're going to be sisters-in-law?"

"You already know the answer to that question. But I'm afraid for you," her voice shook. "Joana has always loved my brother. That's the underlying reason why her marriage didn't work. I would hate to see you destroyed by Rafael's indifference. He has never been able to love anyone but Isabell."

"I'm aware of that. We're only going to stay married until he finds a replacement for Maria, but that could take time."

"Oh Mallory—I'm worried for you. Please don't think me cruel, but I have my reasons for my doubts. You might as well know that I remained fat through most of college until I fell in love with a man named Mateus who came to work at the palacio. For the first time in my life I starved myself to get thin so he would pay attention to me.

"When he did, we spent every moment together and he proposed. I went to Rafael and told him we were going to be married. I thought he'd be happy for me. Instead he asked to speak to Mateus alone.

"The next thing I knew, Mateus had left the palacio and virtually disappeared. When I demanded to know what had happened, Rafael said he told Mateus that if he married me, that was fine as long as he realized I wouldn't be receiving any kind of inheritance. Mateus would have to support me on his own.

"I couldn't believe Rafael had done such a thing but he was testing Mateus. Worse, I couldn't bear it that Mateus didn't love me enough to marry me anyway. I had assumed that losing weight was the only obstacle to getting what I wanted. It was the most ghastly experience of my whole life.

"At one point I stopped eating altogether, not caring if I died. Rafael put me in the hospital and insisted I receive professional help."

"Thank heaven he did, Lianor!" Mallory cried. At last she had the explanation she'd been waiting for. "I'm sorry you've been through so much pain."

"Don't be. It's been over for a long time and I learned a valuable lesson. You can't make another person love you. It isn't possible. I don't want you to suffer the way I did.

"I know you and Apolonia care for each other a great deal, but my brother has been closed off emotionally since Isabell's death. He can be a very hard man. I can't bear it if he hurts you."

He can be gentle too. And loving, and exciting.

Mallory had seen that side of him over the last two days when he'd let down his guard to enjoy Disneyland with Apolonia.

"I know what I'm doing, Lianor."

"But you're giving up your career—"

Mallory got out of the chair and started pacing. "To take on a much more important one.

It's what I want to do. Then I'll come back to California.''

That was the speech she'd given Rafael. She would stick to it until he begged her to be his wife in the true sense of the word.

''Does my brother know that?''

''Yes. We talked everything out tonight. I'm going to sublet my condo so I'll have a place to come home to when I leave his employ. He wanted a nanny, and that's what he's going to get. Nothing more, nothing less.'' But only for the time being.

''Will that really be enough for you?''

No. But she wasn't about to divulge her master plan to anyone. ''I guess I'm going to find out. Lianor? Do me a favor?''

''Anything.''

''If you should hear from Rafael before we arrive in Lisbon, let him know we've talked and that you understand the situation for what it really is. In case you were wondering, Apolonia's the one who suggested we marry in order to satisfy convention.''

''Somehow that doesn't surprise me,'' Lianor murmured. ''I've never seen her so determined about anything in my life. She adores you.''

''I'm crazy about her too. No matter what else the world is going to think, at least there'll be honesty between the four of us. That's all that is important.''

''No it's not all, but I'll be quiet now because I have my own selfish reasons for being overjoyed that you're going to become my sister-in-law.''

''Thank you, Lianor. I feel the same way about you.'' She cleared her throat. ''Your brother wants us to be married in the chapel at the palacio. Will you be my maid of honor?''

''I'd be thrill—oh, someone else is trying to ring me.''

''Maybe it's Rafael. I'll say goodnight. We'll see you Monday.''

After clicking off, Mallory phoned her parents. They would probably tell her she was making the biggest mistake of her life, but it didn't matter. The thought of life without Rafael and Apolonia was no life at all.

* * *

Once Mallory's parents and Liz had hugged her, Violente's daddy was the first person to congratulate her on her marriage.

Rafael had opened the great dining room of the palacio for their wedding reception. She could hardly believe the nightmarish scene in front of her condo three weeks ago had ever taken place.

Luis smiled at her. "Senhora D'Afonso— you have no idea what great pleasure it gives me to call you that. Carolina and I are so happy for you and Rafael. May your marriage be blessed with more children for our children to play with."

Rafael was busy talking to Violente's mother. If her new husband heard the remark, he didn't react.

"I think Rafael has taken on about as much as he can handle right now," she quipped.

"He's a very fortunate man."

"I'm the one who's fortunate, Luis. Perhaps you and Carolina would be willing to let Violente take tennis lessons with me and Apolonia this summer. I'm going to sign us up after we get back from our honeymoon."

She'd found out through Lianor that Rafael had been the star player for his college tennis team. He still played with his friends on occasion. After hearing that bit of news, Mallory thought it would be fun if she and Apolonia learned the fundamentals. Why not surprise him? It would be an activity the three of them could share.

She also planned to give Apolonia lessons on using a surfboard. Rafael had taught his daughter to be an excellent swimmer. If she learned how to surf too, she'd be able to have more fun in the ocean and handle herself with even greater confidence.

Luis's brows furrowed. ''It won't be much of a honeymoon if you're taking Apolonia with you.''

If Mallory had her way, there would be a true honeymoon one day. But not yet... Probably not for a long time if the chaste kiss Rafael had given her at the altar was anything to go by. He couldn't have made it more clear that he was not a husband on fire for his new bride.

"Apolonia's still fragile now that Maria's gone. I think it best to keep her with us until she has passed through the worst of her grief. Rafael agrees."

It was decided they would make a three-day trip to one of the pousadas Rafael owned further north. Apolonia hadn't seen it, nor had Mallory of course. They would do some sightseeing en route. In fact they were leaving as soon as the reception was over.

Luis studied her for a long moment. "You truly love her don't you."

She swallowed hard. "From the beginning."

"Between your beauty, and your love for Apolonia, it's no mystery why Rafael hasn't been able to resist you."

Oh but he has, Luis. Now more than ever.

Since their flight to Lisbon, Rafael had ensconced her in one of the palacio's guest rooms, and had been treating her like he did Lianor. And he would go on resisting her until she found a way to make him fall in love with her. They were in a war with only their first battle behind them.

"You've talked to her too long, Luis. It's my turn."

Carolina hugged Mallory. Whispering in her ear she said, "Every woman in Portugal is in mourning today, but I have to tell you I am as excited as my daughter over your marriage to Rafael.

"Violente is crazy about you. She was so overjoyed to be asked to be a flower girl, she hasn't slept for days! Just look at our girls!"

Our girls.

Already Mallory felt a special camaraderie with Carolina who was four years older. "They're adorable aren't they."

Both of them wore beautiful floor-length white dotted-swiss dresses like Lianor's. All three were crowned with garlands of pink, lavender and white flowers.

It was a fairy-tale wedding with Rafael looking so dashing in his black tuxedo, he was the cynosure of every female eye. Mallory had to practice the greatest self-control not to stare at him throughout the reception.

Apolonia had shown her pictures of her parents' wedding day. They'd been married at

Isabell's family church in Sintra. She had been a petite bride with short, curly black hair who wore ivory satin with cap sleeves and a floor-length veil.

It pleased Mallory that Rafael had wanted their marriage to take place at the palacio. She'd purposely worn her hair long beneath her mother's shoulder-length veil. The silk dress was a round-necked, simple A-line with sheer lace sleeves to the wrists, all of it shocking white.

The two brides couldn't have looked more different. No doubt Rafael was remembering his first wedding when he'd been madly in love with Apolonia's mother.

Mallory recognized there was a part of him that would always treasure her memory, but that was ten years ago. Mallory was his wife now. Though their marriage had taken place to ensure his daughter's happiness at the most vulnerable time in her life, Mallory had another agenda. All she had to do was be patient.

''Senhora D'Afonso?'' Rafael's best man, Antonio, claimed her attention, breaking in on her reverie.

For the next hour she greeted the rest of their guests, many of whom wanted to entertain her and Rafael after they returned from their honeymoon.

Just the mention of the word reminded her that a passion-filled wedding night with her new husband would pass her by. That knowledge prevented her from eating much of the delicious feast Felipe had prepared in their honor. Not so Rafael who appeared to enjoy his meal to the fullest.

Mallory had arranged ahead of time for Apolonia to sit between her and Rafael at the long banquet table. Lianor sat at her brother's side with Antonio and his wife. The Ellises and Liz were placed next to Mallory.

When the photographer came to the table telling them to pose, Rafael put his arm around his daughter and Mallory. No one watching would guess they weren't an ecstatically happy family. From all the smiles of the well-wishers, his behavior convinced the guests that theirs was a real love match.

When the final pictures were taken, he leaned behind Apolonia's back to get Mallory's attention. ''Shall we get going?''

She nodded. ''Come on, Apolonia. Let's hurry upstairs and change our clothes.''

Rafael helped them from the table and escorted them through the closest set of double doors leading to the private staircase.

All Mallory's personal belongings had been transferred to the master suite. Except for the outfits they were going to wear for the rest of the day, everything for their trip had been packed in Rafael's sleek black car.

The week before the wedding Lianor had taken the girls shopping to her favorite stores. Among several things they'd bought were a becoming navy cotton top with matching skirt for Apolonia, and a three-piece silk suit in peppermint pink for Mallory. She wanted Rafael to be proud of them.

Judging by the glint of admiration in his eyes as they appeared in the foyer of the palacio, they hadn't disappointed him. He'd also changed out of his tux and was sporting a summer suit in a tan color that highlighted his dark, handsome looks.

Needing to do something with all the pent-up energy he incited without being aware of it, Mallory did the traditional American thing and threw her bouquet to Lianor. She caught it and blew Mallory a kiss.

To her surprise Rafael grabbed her around the waist and rushed her out the massive doors. The guests followed them down the steps to the car where the photographer continued to take pictures.

While Mallory waved to her parents, Apolonia called to Violente from the back seat window.

"I'll phone you as soon as we get back."

"What's wrong with Violente?" Mallory asked as Rafael drove them away. "She looks like she's crying."

"Her papa got mad at her for asking if she could come with us."

"I should think so," Rafael muttered.

Mallory blinked. "Would you like her to come? It's not too late for your father to turn the car around."

Even from the small distance separating their bucket seats she felt him stiffen.

"No. I just want to be with you and papa. Do you think Maria saw the wedding today?"

Rafael made a strange sound in his throat. "I'm sure she did."

"I hope so. It will make her happy to know I have a new mother, even if you are an American."

A chuckle escaped Mallory's lips. "Are we so terrible?"

"No. Maria didn't like foreigners, but she would have loved you, wouldn't she Papa."

"After Mallory saved you in the ocean, I have no doubt of it."

They were headed north along the coast and couldn't have driven more than a mile further before Apolonia said, "Now that we're a family, can I call you mama?"

CHAPTER EIGHT

MALLORY bowed her head.

The question was one she hadn't been expecting. Not when Apolonia knew the real reason for their marriage.

She darted Rafael a covert glance. His closed expression gave nothing away. What did he expect her to say? What did he *want* her to say?

"If it's all right with your father, nothing would thrill me more, darling."

"Good," Apolonia said as if Rafael had already spoken. "When I go back to school, I'll be like all the other girls whose mothers help the nuns take us on trips. Maria never did because lots of students made her nervous."

Mallory could understand that. "What kind of places do you visit?"

"Churches and museums around Lisbon and other towns."

"On a bus?"

"Yes."

"That sounds fascinating. My school used to do the same thing."

"Where did you go?"

"Oh...let me think. To an observatory and a nuclear reactor plant. Sometimes we toured a film studio."

"I wish our school did things like that."

"Other places always sound more fun, Apolonia, but the truth is you live in a country so full of history, it would take a lifetime to absorb it all. Do you have any idea how lucky you are to come from such a fabulous heritage?

"I'm only beginning to understand just how fabulous. While I'm taking care of you, I'm going to learn all I can. Will you teach me Portuguese?"

"Yes."

"How do you say, wonderful?"

"*Admiravel.*"

Mallory tried it out. After three attempts Rafael told her she pronounced it perfectly. Those were the first words he'd spoken in the last fifteen minutes.

"Where is the pousada we're staying in to-night?"

He flicked her an enigmatic glance. "Obidos. We won't reach it till dark."

She was so attracted to him, she felt a strange sweet pain in the palms of her hands. "Tell me about the town."

"It's a charming village with a cluster of whitewashed houses on a hill enclosed within the walls of a Medieval castle. The interior is crisscrossed by ancient alleys and walkways. The Pousada D'Afonso is a former nunnery built in the Fourteenth Century. You'll find it rather stark."

"I can't wait to see it. I bet it's full every night."

His white smile changed the rhythm of her heart. "That's the idea."

She watched his strong hands on the steering wheel as he maneuvered the car with unconscious expertise. The new gold wedding band on his ring finger gleamed in the fading light. It hit her so hard that this magnificent man was her husband, she could hardly draw breath.

"Lianor told me you're one of the most successful businessmen in Portugal. When I saw the palacio in broad daylight, I realized why."

His dark gaze played over her once more. "Don't leave me hanging. Not after a comment like that."

In this slightly teasing mood, he was irresistible. "You didn't add a swimming pool or tennis courts to ruin the ambience. The discriminating tourist wants authenticity, not commerciality.

"To me Portugal is like a crown of precious jewels. You wouldn't want one stone to lose its brilliance or be removed from its setting. That's what would happen in the wrong developer's hands."

She heard a sharp intake of breath.

"After Lady Windemere has installed a new vice president, how would you like to work with me part-time?"

Was he serious?

Her heart began to thud. "In what capacity?"

"Scouting for new properties with an eye to potential markets."

Under any other circumstances Mallory would be flattered. But this was the man she'd just married! She wanted to be a real Portuguese wife to him, to stay home and take care of him and his daughter. To cook for him. She wanted to have his baby.

"I imagine I'll be too busy taking care of Apolonia to do anything that time-consuming." She looked over her shoulder before saying in a hushed voice, "Since she has fallen asleep, now might be the best time to talk to you about getting a dog."

The car seemed to accelerate. "Where did that come from?"

"While we were at Camp Snoopy she told me she always wanted a dog, but you said no because Maria couldn't abide animals. I found out she threatened to leave if Apolonia acquired one."

"That's true," he muttered. "She had an irrational dislike of pets, so I didn't push it for fear of offending her."

"Well I happen to adore dogs and had one while I was growing up. Because I was an only child, it was the closest thing to a sibling.

Apolonia's the perfect age to get one and be responsible for it. I would help her train it.''

''That's a lot of work.''

''I know, but we have two months before Apolonia's back in school. The other day I looked up the names of some breeders on the Internet and found out there's a kennel in Lisbon that sells beagles. I thought it would be fun if we surprised her by stopping there on our way home.

''You know what they say.'' She smiled at him. ''Acquiring a dog may be the only opportunity a human ever has to choose a relative.''

His black gaze trapped hers. ''In case you've forgotten, Apolonia chose you.''

Mallory hadn't forgotten.

''Does that mean you're against the idea of a dog?''

He shook his dark head. ''Not at all. When I was a boy, our family had several. Since our return from California I've been thinking about getting her one myself. However I had planned to broach the subject with you after we got back from Obidos.''

"I'm so glad you want her to have one. It doesn't have to be a beagle of course."

"No, but a short hair doesn't take as much grooming and a beagle would be a good size for her. Not to mention the fact that she's been asking for a real live Snoopy every night in her prayers."

Mallory hadn't been aware of that fact, yet she wasn't surprised. Apolonia knew her way around her father like nobody's business.

"Now that we have that settled, I want to hear what *you* would like for a wedding present," he said in a quiet voice.

Her heart hammered out a savage tattoo. "You gave me one when you let me be her nanny." He'd also turned over Maria's car to her.

A stillness surrounded them.

"I think we graduated way beyond that particular appellation today," he ground out. "She already thinks of you as her new mama."

"Do you mind?" Mallory whispered.

"If I did, it's too late now."

His words found their mark, stabbing her where it hurt so much she had to bite her lip to keep from crying out in pain.

"Don't get up, Jose." The manager of the Obidos pousada was always anxious to please.

"Is there something I overlooked? When you told me Apolonia would be coming with you, I had the love seat moved out and a hide-a-bed sofa put in the room for her."

Rafael had noticed, only it wouldn't be his daughter who'd be sleeping on it.

"Relax, Jose. Everything's perfect, especially the meal you provided. My family finds this place so fascinating, they've gone exploring. I decided it would be a good time to come down and thank you personally for all the trouble you've gone to."

In truth he'd felt it would be less awkward for Mallory if she and Apolonia had a chance to get ready for bed before he returned to the pousada's honeymoon suite.

"My wife loved the snifter of floating gardenias. You had no way of knowing they're her favorite flower. Thank you."

Jose beamed. "It was my pleasure, believe me. Congratulations on your marriage. Senhora D'Afonso is a beautiful woman. Just watching her interact with your charming daughter earlier, it's obvious they care for each other very much. How fortunate for you."

"They went through an experience that bonded them for life." When he told Jose about Apolonia's near drowning and miraculous rescue, the other man sobered.

"That explains their closeness over such a short period of time. As for you..." He suddenly grinned. "Love at first sight, eh?"

Rafael averted his eyes. Not exactly. It was more like 'shock' at first sight. He would never forget watching the woman he'd resented with every fiber of his being emerge from the ocean like some breathtaking mermaid, carrying his unconscious daughter to the beach where she brought her back to life.

He couldn't pinpoint the exact moment when love had come to him. All he knew was that it had happened with the impact of the great tsunami of Lisbon when 30,000 inhabitants had died in fifty-foot-high waves.

Though she might be in love with someone else, she was Rafael's wife now. Possession was nine-tenths of the law. All that remained was to accomplish a takeover of her heart. He wasn't above using any means at hand to achieve his objective.

"Will you want breakfast in your room?"

"No. We'll come down to the dining room. Apolonia can't wait to eat in the refectory where the nuns used to assemble. She's completely fascinated by the subject."

"So was I as a young man, but not for the same reason as your daughter, of course."

Rafael chuckled. "I hear you. *Boa noite, Jose.*"

His manager's comment stayed with him all the way back to the suite. He used the card key to let himself in the room. Only the alcove light had been left on. He tiptoed inside the room. It looked like his daughter was asleep on one side of the king-size bed.

He turned his head and saw Mallory under the covers of the Hide-A-Bed, safe and secure as any mother superior who'd once inhabited this room. If she was still awake, she would never own up to it.

That was all right. Their unorthodox honeymoon was a time for him to practice patience. Once they were back home on his turf, things would change in a big way.

"I wish we didn't have to go home today. I've had the best time of my whole life."

Rafael shot Mallory a covert glance. She could tell he was as excited as she was about stopping at the kennel. Apolonia had no idea what was in store for her.

They'd circled back to Lisbon via a picturesque road from Obidos and had reached one of the residential areas without her even noticing.

"That's what you said after we'd been to Disneyland, *querida*."

Mallory looked over her shoulder at her. "I feel the same way, darling. All the times we've been together have been best, haven't they."

"Yes. I wish you didn't ever have to work, Papa."

His deep-bodied laughter rang out in the car. Mallory had heard it a lot over the last three days while they'd explored Obidos. She never wanted it to stop.

He sounded happy.

She hoped her presence had something to do with this change in him, and not solely because he'd found a permanent replacement for Maria.

"How come we're stopping here?"

They'd pulled up in front of a private residence.

"Do you see that sign on the house?" her father asked.

"Yes."

"Why don't you translate it for Mallory."

"But I don't know what it means."

Rafael smiled before saying something in Portuguese. Suddenly there was a surprised gasp from Apolonia. "They sell dogs here?"

"Yes, *querida.* Very special dogs called beagles."

After a moment of silence, *"Snoopy?"* she blurted with joy.

His laughing eyes captured Mallory's. Her heart felt like it was going to burst from the love she yearned to shower on him.

Apolonia was out of the car and running toward the house before Rafael could catch up to her. By the time Mallory reached them, he'd already tugged on the bellpull.

A middle-aged man answered the door and told them to walk around the back.

They complied and found a small building behind his residence. He met them, then opened the door to the kennel where he introduced his wife.

She was inside a large cage with a mother beagle and two little beagles. The man said something in Portuguese to Rafael who translated.

"They've sold all of the litter except these two. The bigger one is the last female. They're weaned and have had their shots, but the runt is still attached to his mother."

"What's a runt, Papa?"

"The smallest one," her father explained.

"Oh...he's so cute!" Apolonia cried. "Can I hold him?"

"The female will be easier to raise."

"But I want *him.*"

Everyone smiled as the woman opened the door of the cage and carefully handed the wriggling little white and tan pup to Apolonia. The mother didn't like it one bit and began moaning.

Apolonia put it against her shoulder and petted it while she made crooning sounds. Her maternal instincts were already out in full force. When her eyes looked up, Mallory saw those stars in them again. She'd made her choice.

"I'm going to call him Flash."

A shocked gasp came out of Mallory.

"Flash?" Her father couldn't have looked more perplexed.

"It means lightning, doesn't it, Mama?"

Mama.

"Yes," she answered in a shaky voice. *Just don't say anything else. Please, Apolonia.*

"Well," Rafael muttered in a resigned voice, "I guess this is the one we want." Then he reverted to Portuguese while he and the man did business. His wife found a box with a top to take the puppy home in. It cried like a human.

Apolonia tried to soothe it all the way to the car. Mallory walked next to her.

"Why won't he stop crying?"

"Because he has never left his mother before, but he'll get over it in a few days. We'll drive to a pet store and buy everything he needs."

The puppy squealed in such ear-screeching decibels, Rafael was only too eager to do the shopping.

"Be sure to get a little floor heater," Mallory reminded him before he levered himself from the car. She stayed behind to help Apolonia console the frightened little thing.

When Rafael came out of the store, his arms were loaded with a doggie bed and a huge sack full of stuff.

"I feel like we've just had a baby," he grumbled after he'd put everything in the trunk and was back at the wheel.

"We have," Mallory teased.

He let out a sound between a laugh and a cry.

Their peaceful three day sojourn had come to an abrupt end. It would be chaos from here on out. Mallory loved it. She loved this new life so much it terrified her.

It was growing dark by the time they drew up in front of the palacio a half hour later. The puppy's wails could be heard all over the beach. Scarcely a word passed between Rafael and the surprised staff who'd come outside to help with their bags.

"We'll put the puppy on the balcony for now," he said to Apolonia who clutched the box in her hands. Mallory grabbed the doggie bed while Rafael carried the sack. The three of them rushed inside the palacio and up the private staircase to the master suite.

Within a few minutes the balcony resembled a kennel of sorts. A very elegant kennel in a royal palace with every necessity a dog needed including a kong and a ball that played music as it rolled.

Doggie treats, puppy chow, a spray to disinfect, a finger toothbrush and a collar and leash now decorated the table where they'd once eaten the fabulous meal Felipe had prepared.

Mallory was secretly thrilled that Rafael's instincts had been to keep the puppy close to Apolonia. She'd already taken it out of the box. They watched it wander around where Rafael had laid paper toweling.

In a few minutes Mallory ran to the bathroom and filled one of the bowls with water. After placing it next to the balcony wall, she poured some puppy chow into the other bowl and put it by the water.

"There's your food, Flash. Come on." Apolonia picked up the puppy and set him down next to the bowls, but the unhappy little thing just kept crying.

"Why don't you sit down right there and put a little chow in your palm. Pretty soon he'll catch on," Mallory suggested.

In a second Apolonia started to giggle. "Flash's tongue tickles."

"You see, *querida?* He's already getting to know you and trust you."

Her father got down on his haunches next to her. "How did you ever come up with a name like Flash?"

Uh-oh.

"It's the name of the man Mallory loves," Apolonia confided while she concentrated all her attention on the puppy. "He lives in Hollywood!"

Rafael's solid body seemed to freeze before he turned his head and looked up at Mallory. There was no light in his eyes now. They were black as pitch.

"That's one of the more unusual American names I've ever heard."

She sensed that his not-so-subtle sarcasm covered another emotion. Was he upset by the idea that she loved someone else? If that were true…

Mallory's heart took off running.

"He's a very unusual man."

"He *is,* Papa. Mama showed me a picture of him. He's powerful, like lightning." She kissed her puppy's head. "I don't care if you're the runt, Flash. One day you're going to be powerful too and—oh!'' She laughed. ''He just wet all over me!''

That started Mallory chuckling, but she noticed Rafael didn't join in.

''Time for a bubble bath young lady. We'll let your father deal with Flash.''

Without waiting for a response from him, she put the puppy in Rafael's hands, then ushered Apolonia through the suite to the bathroom in her own bedroom.

''While you bathe and wash your hair, I'm going to take a shower and get ready for bed too, darling. Then we'll say goodnight to the puppy.''

''I wish he could sleep with me.''

''One day he will when he's been trained.''

''How long do you think it'll take?''

''Several months at least.''

''I love him so much.''

''He's awfully cute.''

She picked up Apolonia's soiled clothes and put them in the hamper before returning to the master bedroom. In one of the dresser drawers lay a modest lavender cotton nightgown and matching robe Liz had given her. Draping them over her arm she wandered into Rafael's bathroom.

Since the three of them had shared the same bathroom in Obidos, Mallory didn't feel at all strange taking a shower in here for the first time. Technically speaking, this was her bedroom and bathroom too.

It smelled of his soap and shampoo, the shaving cream he used. She took great pleasure putting her own cosmetics and hairbrush on the inlaid tile counter next to his things.

A striped bathrobe she hadn't seen before hung on the hook of the bathroom door. She placed her new nightwear over it while she showered and washed her hair.

This was no longer his sole domain. A smile broke out on her face. If it was jealousy she'd felt coming from him a little while ago, hopefully the invasion of her things in his inner sanctum would haunt him until one day he cracked wide open.

Ten minutes later she joined him on the balcony, still drying her hair with a towel. Now that it was July, the nights were soft and balmy. The only light reflected from the bedroom. She found him lounging against the wall while he let the puppy lick his fingers from his new doggie bed.

Mallory enjoyed watching their interaction so much, she hated to disturb such a touching scene. But since she was the one who'd brought up the subject of buying a puppy in the first place, she needed to do her part.

''The bathroom's free, Rafael. I'll take over now if you want.''

He lifted his head. She felt a trail of fire as his gaze traveled from her bare feet, up her body to her face.

''I'm in no particular hurry to move,'' he murmured. ''Come and sit with me.''

If he'd been upset earlier, there was no sign of it now. A wave of heat engulfed her.

She closed the distance between them and started to kneel down in front of the little bed. But she didn't make it all the way because Rafael's strong arms pulled her onto his lap. The towel slid away.

''Isn't this more comfortable than the stone floor?'' he whispered into her damp hair.

Unable to speak, let alone breathe while her back lay against his broad chest, her body pulsated like a hot blue star in the firmament.

One of his hands returned to the puppy who'd settled down. The other caressed the skin of her arm below her sleeve, sending tiny darts of yearning through her system.

"You smell sweet like that field of wildflowers we drove through yesterday. I'm becoming addicted to your scent."

Her heart thudded. "Perhaps now you understand why Lady Windemere products are selling so well."

"I'm talking about you…your skin…your hair. You're incredibly beautiful, Mallory. Ever since you warned me that I wouldn't find you lying in wait for me on my bed one dark lonely night in the hope of trapping me, I haven't been able to erase that provocative picture from my mind."

He swept some of her hair aside to kiss her nape. "Would it surprise you if I told you I want you in my bed?"

She drew in lungfuls of air. "No. You've been alone ten years. You're a normal male with normal needs, and now you've married again, cutting yourself off from your former girlfriends. Nothing could be more natural than to turn to me, even if our wedding was meant to serve as a front.''

His hand slid to her shoulder, kneading it with growing insistence. ''If you're telling me you're not attracted to me, then you're lying. I can feel your pulse throb wherever I touch you.''

She couldn't swallow. ''You're a very exciting man, Rafael. I'd have to be made of stone not to find you desirable.''

''Your honesty takes my breath.'' She felt his hands move around her hips, drawing her even closer against him. ''I want to make love to you, Mallory. I've wanted it for a long time,'' he admitted in a husky voice. ''Tonight will be our true wedding night.''

It wasn't a declaration of love, and he wasn't asking for a similar declaration in return, but it was a beginning of sorts. He believed she loved someone else, so he felt safe in reaching out for a night of passion.

Though she could never give her body if she didn't love a man heart and soul, she knew Rafael could separate his heart from pure physical need.

Since he was prepared to act on that need tonight, she would follow her business instincts and seize the moment. Otherwise there might not be another invitation from him and he'd find comfort in someone else's arms. She couldn't afford to let that happen!

"I'll come to you after Apolonia has fallen asleep," she promised before easing herself out of his arms. He seemed reluctant to let her go.

No sooner had she stood up than his pajama-clad daughter came running out to the balcony holding a brush and elastic. She knelt down and kissed the puppy first, oblivious to Mallory's inner elation.

"Did you miss me?" The attention woke it up. "I'm back, and I'm going to stay next to you all night."

By now Rafael had gotten to his feet. "I'm afraid not, *querida*. He needs to learn to sleep on his own."

"But Papa—"

"No buts."

"Let me do your hair before you go to bed," Mallory urged with an excitement she could scarcely hide.

Apolonia picked up the puppy and held it while Mallory fashioned a ponytail. "There you go."

Her father plucked the puppy from her shoulder and put him back in his bed. "Come on. I'll listen to you say your prayers."

"But what if Flash cries for me?"

"He has to get used to being alone."

Mallory hugged her. "Just remember he'll be waiting for you in the morning. You'll have all day to play with him. We'll invite Violente to come over."

"When she sees Flash she'll want a puppy just like him," she chatted as Rafael ushered her into the bedroom. The knowledge that he was so anxious to get Apolonia to bed set Mallory's body trembling.

She put the brush on the table, then walked to the edge of the balcony where she could watch the foaming surf. The soft breeze was cooler now. Too cool for their new little puplet.

"Come on, Flash." She picked up his bed and put it in a dark corner of the bedroom. He whined. "Be a good boy and go to sleep." After a few minutes of petting him, he settled down once more on top of the washable pad.

Feverish with anticipation for the moment when Rafael joined her, she hurried into the bathroom to blow-dry her hair. It didn't take long before it floated like a cloud over her shoulders.

She emerged at the same time she saw Rafael turn the key in the lock of the door separating them from Apolonia's room. The sound of the click got buried in the heavy pounding of her heart.

Now that they were alone, she could almost hear the crackle of static electricity surrounding them.

He moved toward her with the stealth of a dark jungle cat.

"Wait for me," he whispered against her lips without touching her anywhere else. "I won't be long."

After he'd disappeared into the bathroom, she touched the lips he'd set on fire.

She nearly collapsed from weakness on her way to the bed. The covered buttons of her robe were almost impossible to undo with such shaky fingers.

This wasn't just her wedding night. This would be her first time with a man period!

Until she'd lost weight, she'd stayed clear of guys, especially the one she'd always wanted to be her boyfriend. By the time she gained her confidence, he'd disappeared from the scene and it was too fun dating one guy after another to think of getting physical.

At Yale she'd sensed the men who came on to her were frustrated academicians. They were into some kind of male upsmanship thing, hoping to score with her. The result being that her distrust of their motives prevented her from falling in love. Without the involvement of her deepest emotions, she would never go to bed with a man.

Since working for Liz, she only dated on occasion. Dinner and a movie, that kind of thing. Rafael could have no idea how innocent she was, but it didn't matter. What she lacked in personal experience, she more than made up for by loving him to distraction.

After a debate over what to do, she finally removed her robe and climbed in his bed. As she pulled the covers over her, he came out of the bathroom. In that split second before he turned off the light, she noticed he'd put on the striped robe.

The next instant he'd slid beneath the quilt and reached for her. *"Por deus, amada—"* he cried softly. "Come closer. Give me your luscious mouth."

Before she knew how it happened, she was half lying on top of him, responding to the fierce hunger of his kiss with an eagerness she couldn't control. There was no question of them taking things slow. They were both on fire for each other.

Mallory had never known sensations like this before. Every touch of his hands and mouth thrilled her until she moaned in pleasure. The world was slipping away to a place she'd never been.

"Rafael—" she cried helplessly when he finally allowed her to take a breath.

"I know exactly how you feel," came his ragged response. He reversed their positions so his face hovered over hers, their legs and arms entangled. She didn't want him that far away from her and pulled his head down again.

No kiss was long enough, deep enough. She felt herself swirling faster and faster into a vortex of such ecstasy, her body shook with the passion he'd aroused.

Just then they heard sounds of wailing nonstop like a newborn baby.

The puppy!

In her rapturous state, she'd forgotten all about him.

Rafael groaned in protest before he tore his lips from hers and sat up to listen. "It sounds like he's in our bedroom."

"He is," she confessed. "I brought him in while you were showering because I was afraid he'd get too cold out on the balcony during the night."

When they heard another sound coming from the connecting door, both their heads turned in its direction.

"Papa? I can't get in! My puppy needs me!"

Rafael pressed a hard kiss to Mallory's mouth, then he slid out of bed, retying the belt of his robe.

"I'll take care of him, *querida*," he called to his daughter. "You go back to bed."

"You can't expect her to do that, Rafael. Not now." Mallory tossed back the covers and got to her feet, straightening her nightgown. "While you let her in, I'll get the floor heater."

She turned on the bedside lamp so she could find her robe. It had fallen to the floor in a heap. After she put it on, she hurried out to the balcony and pulled it from the sack.

After she'd gone back in the bedroom and had plugged it in so the heat and sound of the motor would give comfort to the puppy, Rafael opened the door.

Apolonia rushed in. She reached for her unhappy pet and put him against her shoulder.

"Don't cry, Flash. I'm here." She darted her father a vexed glance.

"How come you locked the door, Papa?"

"Yes, Senhor D'Afonso," Mallory spoke up with as straight a face as she could muster. "Why did you?"

Rafael's black eyes sent her a private message that said she would pay for that when he got her to himself again.

She couldn't wait!

But it looked like she was going to have to.

"Mallory and I needed to discuss something important in private, *querida.*"

Heat flamed Mallory's cheeks. Though the disappointment at being interrupted had almost killed her, maybe it was good that fate had conspired to stop them before things had gone any further.

Once again Mallory was reminded of the words that had been her secret guide for a long time.

Women are the nature-endowed soldiers of Aphrodite, goddess of love and beauty, and theirs is the only conquering army to which men will permanently submit—not only with-

out resentment or resistance or secret desires
for revenge, but also with positive willingness
and joy!

It was the *permanent* part she was after, not
just one night. This evening she'd been his for
the taking, like a ripe plum. But she couldn't
help it if he'd only been allowed a nibble because outside circumstances had interfered.

Perhaps if he were forced to wait a little
while before he took his next bite, it would
prey on his mind day and night until his every
thought was of her. She wanted him to come
running over and over again for the rest of
their lives because he couldn't help himself.

"I tell you what, darling." She put a hand
on Apolonia's shoulder. "Why don't we let
your father deal with Flash tonight? Tomorrow
night we'll put the puppy in your room and
take care of him. Pretty soon he'll get used to
living here and won't cry anymore. All right?"

"I guess." After a dozen more kisses to its
adorable head she put him back on the pad.
"*Boa noite,* Papa."

"*Boa noite,* Rafael," Mallory called over
her shoulder before following his daughter

through the connecting door. She heard him whisper her name, but she didn't dare turn around or she would run back to his bed.

Better to leave him wanting, even if it meant she laid awake all night remembering what it was like to lie in his arms for a little while and be kissed senseless.

CHAPTER NINE

MALLORY wasn't surprised when she woke up to discover Apolonia had already left the bedroom. Like a busy mother, she'd run to take care of her precious baby.

In case Flash had kept Rafael awake during the night, he probably welcomed his daughter coming to the rescue. Mallory had tossed and turned for hours.

So many times she'd wanted to slip back to his room, but somehow she'd resisted the impulse and had finally fallen asleep. Now she was left with a permanent ache nothing would take away until they could be alone with no chance of anything disturbing them. That was assuming Rafael hadn't already lost interest...

Almost sick with excitement to see him this morning, she got ready for the day in a pair of white slacks and a sleeveless ribbed top of wide navy and white bands. After tying her hair at the nape with a white chiffon scarf, she slipped on white sandals and hurried through the adjoining door.

Her glance flew to his empty, unmade bed. She kept walking to the balcony where she found Apolonia playing with her puppy. There was no sign of Rafael. Though the sun had burned off most of the mist, his absence took away some of the beauty of the morning for her.

''How's Flash today?''

Apolonia looked up with a smile. ''He's been following me around. Before Papa left for Cabo Espichel, he showed me how to get the puppy to start going to the bathroom on the paper.''

Mallory's heart lurched at the news that Rafael had left the palacio.

''I didn't know he had plans to be away today.'' She'd hoped the three of them could go swimming in the ocean.

''The manager called to tell him there was an emergency. To come quick. Papa said he didn't know when he'd be back.''

''I see,'' she murmured while her mind conjured up a dozen different scenarios serious

enough to require Rafael's immediate presence, none of them good. It was all he'd
needed after being forced to deal with the
puppy for most of the night.

She glanced at her watch, shocked to see it
was almost ten o'clock. Some great nanny she
was turning out to be! The first morning on the
job and everyone had risen long before her.

"Tell you what. There are some things I'd
like to do in Atalaia this morning." Might as
well get a summer routine established now.
"Why don't you phone Violente and see if she
can come over. If her mother says yes, tell her
we'll pick her up. Remind her to bring her
bathing suit."

"I will. Can we take Flash with us?"

"No, darling. He'll be much better off here.
By the time the afternoon sun hits the balcony,
we'll be back."

Apolonia lowered the puppy into his bed.
"He's going to miss me."

Sure enough as soon as Mallory closed the
balcony door, they could hear it start to squeal
again. "I'm sure he will, but he's a baby and
needs lots of naps. We won't be gone long."

After Mallory put Apolonia's hair in a ponytail with a blue scarf to match her shorts and
top, she called her friend from Rafael's bedside phone and arrangements were made.

Mallory collected her purse from the
dresser. ''Shall we grab a bite to eat in the
kitchen first?''

''In the kitchen?''

''Why not?'' They walked down the private
staircase together. ''Haven't you ever done
that before?''

''No. Maria said it wasn't proper.''

''I think it's proper when there's just two of
us and the cooks and waiters are busy taking
care of guests. Don't you?''

''Yes. Mauricio's going to be surprised.''

''Who's Mauricio?''

''He's the morning chef. He's not as nice as
Felipe,'' she confided in a hushed voice, ''and
he doesn't speak English.''

A minute later they entered the huge kitchen
and Mallory found herself the object of the
cooking staff's scrutiny. The large, dark-
skinned chef put her in mind of Shakespeare's

Othello, the man whose jealousy proved to be his downfall.

After Apolonia made the introductions Mallory said, "Ask him if I could scramble some eggs over on that stove he's not using. Tell him we'll be buying groceries to cook our own meals most days from now on."

The girl blinked. "We will?"

"Yes. Cooking's fun. I want to teach you how." The palacio food was too rich and full of calories. "Tell him we promise not to get in his way."

A broad smile broke out on Apolonia's face before she started translating.

A mutinous expression entered his dark brown eyes. It was obvious he didn't like his kitchen being invaded, but she was Rafael's wife. The silence stretched before he said something to one of his assistants who'd been staring at Mallory with blatant male interest.

He walked over. "I'm Eduardo. How can I help?"

"If you would take five minutes to show me where I can keep food I buy for us, where to

find plates, pans and utensils, how to turn on
the stove, I'd be very grateful.''

His eyes smiled. ''Of course. Anything for
Rafael's beautiful new American wife.''

''Thank you. Do you think Mauricio would
mind if we ate on that small table against the
far wall? We'll put our things in the dish-
washer when we're finished if you'll show us
how.''

''That table is never used. You are welcome
to eat there anytime.''

Within fifteen minutes they'd enjoyed a
breakfast of eggs without cheese and cream,
plus fresh fruit which Apolonia helped prepare.
After they'd cleaned up their own mess, she
made a point to thank Mauricio and Eduardo
again before they left for Atalaia.

Maria's car was only a year old, yet it felt
like it was brand new. Apolonia told her where
to drive. Soon they reached Violente's home,
a charming cream-colored villa with purple
bougainvillea everywhere. She came running
outside with a beach bag. Her mom followed,
holding their eleven-month-old.

246 RAFAEL'S CONVENIENT PROPOSAL

The second Mallory saw his dark curly hair, she felt an urgent longing to have Rafael's baby. When she tried to hold him, he clutched his mother's neck.

"I'm sorry, Mallory. He doesn't want anyone but me."

"It's all right. He doesn't know me yet."

"Speaking of babies, are you ready to take the puppy back?"

Mallory chuckled. "Not quite yet, but Rafael might have other ideas. It kept us awake most of the night."

"Tell me about it." Carolina moaned. "I know as soon as Violente sees it, she's going to beg us for one."

"Don't worry. We'll let her share it with Apolonia. Do you think Violente could stay through dinner, then I'll bring her back."

"As long as Rafael doesn't mind."

"He's in Cabo Espichel today."

Carolina frowned. "Away on business so soon?"

"It couldn't be helped. There was an emergency." At least that's what he'd told Apolonia.

All morning Mallory tried to squelch the fear that he'd really gone to be with one of his lovers who'd been missing him for the last month. Someone lovely and available. They would have the whole day to spend without any interruptions.

The pictures that filled Mallory's mind tormented her, especially when she could still feel and taste his mouth. Her body ached to know his possession.

She cleared her throat as if to throw off her demons. "Carolina? Did Luis tell you I would like Violente to take tennis lessons with us this summer?"

"Yes. It's a wonderful idea. I'm afraid this baby has slowed me down so much, I don't seem to have time for anything more demanding right now."

"No wonder. Do you know a place here in Atalaia?"

"There's a public court with a clubhouse two miles down the highway. It'll be on your right. I understand they offer group lessons."

"I'll stop by on our way back to the palacio and see what I can arrange, then I'll phone you. Please keep it a secret. We want to surprise Rafael.''

''I won't say a word.''

''Thank you. See you tonight.''

The girls had already climbed in the back seat and were talking a Portuguese blue streak when Mallory got in the car.

Violente gave explicit directions to the tennis club. It didn't take long to sign them up for the only spots left. Tuesdays and Thursdays from three to four o'clock, the hottest part of the day.

Today was Tuesday. That meant the day after tomorrow would be their first lesson. Mallory would pick up Violente early enough to buy racquets for the three of them.

Two more stops to a market and a store that sold small appliances, then they sped home. While the girls rushed inside to take care of Flash, Mallory put most of the food away in the kitchen. The rest she took to the balcony after asking the front desk if some help could be spared to carry up the mini fridge and microwave she'd bought.

For the next few hours the girls played with the puppy. Mallory heated up some frozen tortillas filled with grilled chicken and vegetables. The girls had never eaten them before. They were a big hit. So were the frozen strawberry yogurts.

Quite a change for Apolonia who'd been consuming nun's bellies and salischa on a regular basis.

So far Rafael hadn't phoned to let her know how long he'd be. When she couldn't stand the suspense any longer she suggested the three of them take a late afternoon swim.

They put Flash in a corner of Apolonia's room and barricaded it before heading down to the beach. The three of them swam within the first curl. Mallory helped them work on their front crawl. Violente was a good little swimmer too.

As for Apolonia, she showed no signs of being afraid of the water since her near drowning experience. The addition of the puppy had helped her focus on something besides herself. It was paying dividends, not only to help her with her confidence, but to give her something on which to lavish her love now that Maria was gone.

Still no phone message from Rafael after they'd returned to the room to shower and change. Apolonia was too enthralled with Flash to ask about her father, but Mallory's disappointment was so unbearable she suggested they leave for Violente's house. En route they could stop at one of those beach kiosks selling seafood meals to go. Anything to get her mind off him.

She found Ines and let her know where they were going in case Rafael arrived home and wondered where they were. A pointless effort as it turned out. When they got back from Atalaia, the housekeeper told them she'd received word he might not be able to make it home till Friday. Something important had come up. There was no special message.

Apolonia took the news in stride. Apparently this was nothing new to her, but Mallory was devastated because he hadn't even tried to call her on the new cell phone he'd bought for her. She could only conclude someone else was keeping him there. Now that he knew his daughter was in safe hands, he could indulge himself without worry.

The brave words she'd once thrown at him came back to haunt her.

Unlike a wife, I won't ask questions about the women you're with when you're away from the palacio. I plan to live my own life taking care of your daughter. I intend to let you live yours.

Once she and Apolonia finally went to bed, she sopped her pillow. It was a good thing the puppy started to howl at the same time. He drowned out the accompanying sobs she fought to silence.

"Alo?"

"Ines—it's Rafael. I finished things up and am on my way home. Any news I should know about?"

"Mauricio is threatening to quit," Ines said.

He blinked. Mauricio— "Why?"

"It's none of my business, but if you wanted to keep the peace, you shouldn't have told Mallory she could do the cooking. Apolonia's been helping her. His feelings are hurt because he thinks she doesn't like the way he prepares the food.

"Since she's been using the microwave and refrigerator she bought to put on the balcony, they don't come down for lunch. I think she's got Apolonia on a healthy eating diet. I'm afraid Felipe's upset too."

It was one of those moments where Rafael didn't know whether to laugh or cry.

Retaining and keeping world-class chefs was vital to his business. But he loved the fact that Mallory had Apolonia's best interests at heart, that she was trying to give his daughter a taste of what family life was all about. It was something that had been missing from his life for so many years. Something he craved with every particle of his being...

"Be assured I'll talk to them, Ines. See you in about an hour."

Rafael couldn't get home fast enough. He'd had to leave the palacio in such a hurry Tuesday morning, he'd gone off without copying down Mallory's new cell phone number. But he'd thought of course Apolonia would call him at some point. Then he would get the number from her.

When she didn't phone, he had to assume that for the moment the puppy dominated her thoughts to the exclusion of everything else. It also meant Mallory couldn't have cared less if she heard from him or not. Otherwise she would have found a way for Apolonia to get in touch with him so she would have an excuse for them to talk.

He knew in his gut her passionate response during those moments in his bed had been genuine. But it terrified him to think she could give herself that way without being in love with him. Could she do that? He recalled a certain conversation with her.

Apolonia told me you're in love with someone and would marry him immediately if he were available.

But he isn't, Rafael. In fact he might never become available. Suffice it to say, Apolonia will be my only priority. I'll add that to the prenuptial agreement so there can be no question of my abandoning her.

It looked like she meant what she'd said.

Rafael took a shuddering breath.

Since he didn't want Ines to suspect that anything was wrong with his marriage, he hadn't tried to phone the palacio again. But it had been two days and nights of hell since he'd held Mallory in his arms. He wouldn't be able to go on living another twelve hours without there being absolute truth between them.

By the time he drove up to the palacio, the sun had started to fall into the ocean. It was a beautiful time of night. All the guests had gone in to dinner leaving the beach deserted.

As he parked the car, he saw something out of the corner of his eye. He couldn't be certain but it looked like a surfboard between the two curls. Surfers were rare along the palacio's private stretch of beach, but if they did come, it was usually at this time of night when the waves were bigger.

He climbed out and took another look.

This time he saw two figures seated on the board while they rode the curl all the way in.

His heart started to vibrate like a jackhammer. It was Mallory and Apolonia! He could hear them whooping with joy.

Without hesitation he stripped down to his boxers, then slipped on some shorts from his suitcase and started running toward the foam.

By this time they'd already started back out to catch another curl. He plunged into the water and propelled himself toward them at tremendous speed. After the strain and tension he'd been under for the last few days, it felt good to expend his energy doing something physical.

Closer now he could see they both wore life preservers. Even a champion surfer like Mallory wasn't taking any chances without a lifeguard around. She did everything right.

He dove beneath the water and came up next to them. "How about making room for me?"

They both cried out in surprise at the same time, but it was Mallory's brilliant blue eyes that spoke to him loud and clear. They didn't lie. She was happy to see him. That was all he needed to know.

"Did you see us ride the wave?" His daughter was having the time of her life.

"I did. It looks like another one is coming."

"Here we go, Apolonia. Hold on tight!" Mallory started paddling.

With a sense of exhilaration, he began swimming alongside them. The three of them caught the curl and rode it all the way in.

When they reached the shallows, Rafael plucked his daughter from the board and hugged her. "I've missed you, *querida*."

"I've missed you too, Papa. I'm so glad you're home."

"So am I."

Mallory stayed on the surfboard watching them.

He carried his daughter to shore and set her down. "Do you mind if I take one ride with Mallory while you wait on the beach for us? Then we'll all go in and see how the puppy's doing."

"He loves me, Papa."

"I have no doubt of it. We'll be back in a minute."

As he swam toward Mallory, his heart did a dropkick when he saw the excitement on her gorgeous face. She turned her surfboard around and lay down on it while she paddled swiftly toward the curls.

Rafael caught up to her. He felt they were shooting for an invisible mark that could change their lives forever. When they'd passed beyond the first curl she turned the surfboard around.

''Did I hear something about you wanting to take a ride?'' she asked in a husky voice. He felt it resonate throughout his system.

''You heard me all right. Here I come.''

He gripped the end of the board and climbed on. The ocean might be cooling off, but the feel of her body against his chest and legs sent a fire raging through him.

She trembled. He knew the reason why... Her desire for him was something she couldn't hide.

When she started to paddle, he caught hold of her arms to still them. ''Not yet,'' he whispered against her neck. ''Let me enjoy being out here alone with you for a few minutes.''

They bobbed up and down. The moment was magical.

He slid his hands around her waist. "I've missed you, *amada.*" Compelled by a force he couldn't control, he buried his lips in her wet hair and kissed her.

"If there'd been any way to get back sooner, I would have. There was a fire in one of the rooms. We didn't know if it had been intentionally set or not. I had to stay until the police finished their investigation. Then I had to hire a company to come in and start repairing the damage. It meant dealing with the insurance company. Everything took time."

"We're glad you're back now. We missed you too."

Her breathless answer wasn't enough for him.

"Apolonia's not here. I want to know if *you* missed me."

"Of course."

"Enough to sleep with me tonight?"

A shiver rocked both their bodies. "I'm not sure that's a good idea."

He sucked in his breath. "Because you're in love with someone else?"

After a brief silence, ''Because Lianor warned me you're still in love with Apolonia's mother.''

That didn't surprise him. She and his sister had grown close long before Mallory ever came to Portugal. No doubt they'd shared certain confidences.

''For a little while the other night I chose to forget that fact. While you've been gone I've had time to consider the situation. Tempted as I am to make love with you, Rafael, I've decided I want my first time to be with a man whose heart is wide open and dying to love me.''

His breath caught in his lungs. She'd never been to bed with a man? That meant she hadn't been intimate with the man she claimed to love.

While he pondered the wonder of it, she leaned forward and started cleaving the water with amazing strength. He felt the swell lift and carry them along the crest of the wave faster and faster. But her revelation caused his spirit to soar ahead of their bodies.

When they came to the shallows, he nibbled her salty earlobe. "Thank you for the ride, *amada*. I'll never forget it," he said before sliding off the board. As they reached the beach he took it from her and carried it beneath his arm.

Apolonia ran up to them. "W—Wasn't that fun, Papa?" She had a towel wrapped around her, but she was shivering.

"It was better than fun, *querida*. Come on. Let's get you inside." He had plans for tonight. The sooner he got his daughter to bed, the sooner he'd be able to carry them out.

They entered the foyer of the palacio. When they passed through the office, Vaz flashed him a welcoming smile.

Just then he felt Apolonia grasp his free hand. "Wait till you see the puppy. He's eating all his food now. I think he's bigger."

"I wouldn't be surprised."

His daughter chattered all the way up the stairs. When they reached his suite, Apolonia ran through to her bedroom. As Mallory headed for the bathroom he said, "After you've had your shower, don't dress for bed. There's something I want to show you.''

''All right,'' she answered in a quiet voice.

The first thing he noticed on the balcony were the new appliances. He rested the surfboard against the wall, then opened the little refrigerator and pulled out a can of pop.

He was so thirsty he took a big gulp before he realized it was a diet drink, the same kind of thing Mallory had served them at her condo in L.A. Rafael craved sugar, but this would have to do for now.

''Look, Papa. Isn't Flash cuter than ever?''

Rafael might only have been gone three days, but the puppy did appear to have grown. He scratched him behind the ears. ''I'll say. Does he still cry for his mother?''

''Yes, but Mallory said it didn't go on as long last night.''

''Good. That means he's starting to feel more at home. Apolonia—before you take your bath, there's a favor I need to ask of you.''

Her brown eyes lifted to his. ''What is it?''

They walked through to her room. "I want tonight to be special for Mallory. Would you mind if Ines slept in here with you? It means you would have to get up with Flash in the night if he cries."

"I want to! Where are you going?"

"If I tell you, you have to promise to keep it a secret from Mallory. She has no idea what I'm planning."

"I won't say anything."

He whispered in her ear.

His daughter smiled her sweetest smile before she put the puppy down and went to her bathroom.

While both women in his life were busy making themselves beautiful, he hurried downstairs to the car to get his suitcase out of the trunk.

On the way back through the office, he drew Vaz aside for a certain conversation. Once that was accomplished he found Ines to obtain her cooperation.

All he had left to do was go to his study and press the history button on his computer. He wanted to see the man Apolonia had tried to show him a month ago.

At the time, jealousy had prevented him from listening to anything about Mallory's lover. But everything had changed since her revelation on the surfboard an hour ago.

CHAPTER TEN

MALLORY couldn't imagine what it was Rafael intended to show her, but she wanted to look her best. After changing her mind several times she settled on the black pantsuit she'd worn the first night of her arrival in Portugal.

She used the blow-dryer on her hair. Again she vacillated about her hairstyle before she decided to leave it loose and flowing.

Rafael had disappeared somewhere. She walked through to Apolonia's room to help her get ready for bed. To her surprise she'd put on pajamas and had already climbed under the covers.

"We've done a lot this week. No wonder you're tired." She sat down on the side of her bed and gave her a kiss on the forehead. "I think you're the most wonderful girl in the world. I love you, Apolonia."

"I love you too, Mama. Thank you for letting me get a dog."

"Don't forget your father wanted you to have one too."

"I know."

"Tonight he told me he needed to show me something. It must be important. I don't know how long it will take. Will you be all right here alone?"

"Ines is going to stay with me until you get back."

Mallory didn't realize Rafael had made formal arrangements. It sounded like they were going to be gone a long time. "I'm glad she'll be here for you. Is there anything I can do for you before we go?"

"I was just going to ask that question."

She turned her head. Rafael had come into the room with Ines. Fresh from the shower, he wore a royal blue sport shirt and tan chinos.

Mallory had never seen him in that color before. His compelling appeal made nonsense of her decision not to get any more physically involved with him. She *was* involved. Every particle and molecule.

He leaned over to kiss his daughter. *"Boa noite, querida."* His glance darted to Mallory, but his eyes were veiled. "Shall we go?"

Whatever was on his mind, he was being very mysterious. "Yes." Her heart raced. When it behaved like that, she felt breathless.

Ines pulled a book from one of the shelves and sat down on the other bed. It looked like she planned to read to Apolonia who waved to Mallory in that special way of hers. She waved back.

How she loved that girl!

"Do I need my purse?" she asked as they walked through to his suite.

"No."

Once they reached the hall, he grasped her hand and didn't let go. To everyone from guest to staff member, they were the master and mistress of the palacio taking a late stroll together before going to bed.

Rafael smiled at people, almost as if he had a secret he was in no hurry to share. Yet his very laid-back demeanor alerted Mallory something profound was going on inside him.

He led her to the other side of the palacio and up the main staircase. The further they advanced down the great corridor, the more her conviction grew that he was taking her to the Alfama suite. Why?

Sure enough they walked all the way to the end. He opened the first set of double doors.

There emblazoned on tiles above the second set of doors was the writing she'd noticed the first night she'd stayed at the palacio.

Our lips meet high easily across the narrow street, was how Lianor had translated them.

Mallory remembered more of their conversation about someone in the D'Afonso family who had romantic notions putting it there. "Most likely it was a man who wanted to remind his wife of her marital duty," Lianor had declared.

Was that what this was all about?

Didn't Rafael know she needed no reminding?

The other night, hadn't he been able to guess she loved him more than life itself?

He pulled the doors shut behind them, then pushed open the doors in front of them and drew her all the way inside.

The magnificence of King Pedro's apartment struck her anew. A thrill of excitement swept through her body to stand in such a historic spot with Rafael.

He *was* a descendent of royalty after all. If he'd been born several hundred years earlier, he would have been a prince. She'd never really thought about that aspect of him until this moment.

When he closed the great doors sealing them inside, her legs began to tremble and her mouth went dry.

They stood a few feet apart in the semidarkness where one lamp burned. He folded his arms.

This might be reality, but she was caught between this world and one of fantasy where the trembling virgin bride had been brought before the prince for his pleasure.

It was a fantasy far more powerful than her childish desire to become an Amazon woman from Paradise Island.

"When I married Isabell we lived with her family in Sintra because she became pregnant right away. She suffered from such severe morning sickness, she spent several months in the hospital on and off being fed intravenously."

"The poor thing," Mallory whispered.

"I couldn't be with her every second because the family business would have fallen apart otherwise. That's when her mother's maid, Maria, was hired to be her personal companion and do any nursing required."

No wonder Maria's death had been so traumatic for him. She'd been an intrinsic part of their lives from the beginning.

"There were times she was so sick, I would have given anything to push back the clock so she wouldn't have become pregnant. When she died of pneumonia because her resistance was so low, I felt as if I was the one responsible for her death."

"Rafael—"

He drew in a ragged breath. "Life was grim for a long time after that because of my parents' death and Lianor's tragic love affair. Did she tell you about it?''

''Yes,'' Mallory whispered.

''Part of Lianor still despises me for exposing Mateus for the opportunist he was.''

''You're wrong, Rafael. You saved her from a lifetime of grief. She loves you so much. You're pretty well all she talked about when she flew to L.A. for training.''

''That's nice to hear,'' he murmured.

''Because it's true!'' Mallory declared.

She watched him rub the back of his neck. ''As you can imagine, the only bright spot in my life has been Apolonia.''

''She's so precious.''

He nodded. ''After Isabell's funeral I brought her and Maria to the palacio. I moved into the bedroom my parents occupied. The room Apolonia sleeps in now was Lianor's. Maria slept in the room I grew up in.''

The picture he painted made Mallory want to cry.

''From that point life just went on. I worked all the hours of the day and night to make the pousada a profitable concern." He looked around.

"My father never could bring himself to open the Alfama suite to tourists, but I knew it would be the palacio's greatest selling point. So I had it renovated at great financial risk.

"As it turns out, it was a risk that paid off. Sheiks, royalty, visiting heads of state were willing to part with a great deal of money to stay in it."

"How was I so lucky?" she interjected.

His slumberous eyes played over her. "Because it meant so much to Lianor."

"She was very blessed to have a brother like you watching over her."

"You think?"

"I *know.*"

He studied her for a long time. "To make a long story short, I recouped my losses in a hurry and made enough money to put a down payment on another pousada."

"And the rest was history," she finished the thought.

His eyes flashed black fire, sending her heart palpitating right out of her chest. "That's right.

It is history, Mallory. All of it. Today I'm a different man. It's a different world.

"Until I watched you carry my daughter out of the water and breathe life back into her, my life had been one of survival and existence. But everything changed at that moment. I knew that love had come into my life again. An earthshaking, soul-destroying kind of love if you couldn't love me back."

Mallory could hardly take it in.

"I fought it, I fought *you,* because your power over me and my daughter was so absolute. I knew what a brilliant attorney you were, that you'd carved out a phenomenal career for yourself.

"Lianor had sung your praises. You were the first person who'd been able to bring my sister back to life after Mateus had gone out of it. Part of me loved you for it, but another part resented you more because I could feel Lianor distancing herself from me.

"We were close growing up. With your arrival, all that seemed to be coming to an end. We were losing Maria."

"I'm so sorry, Rafael."

"If that weren't enough, Apolonia told me you were in love with someone else and would marry him if you could. I felt poleaxed."

Just the way he said the word sent delicious chills up and down her spine.

He moved closer. His eyes swept over her relentlessly. "Why did you allow my daughter to perpetuate the myth that you were in love with some blond, curly haired American? I thought he had to be the one we saw at your condo. That is until I looked on my computer tonight and realized it was *Flash Gordon.*"

Her cheeks flamed. "I can explain."

"I'm listening."

She swallowed hard. "You see—I was showing her Mr. Toad, and then I thought she'd like to see one of my favorite cartoon characters. Up popped a picture of the movie star who played the role of Flash Gordon."

"He's been dead several years I understand."

"Yes, he has. Anyway, I told Apolonia that I'd always wanted to marry him, but he wasn't available. To this day I don't know if she took me literally or not. But when you jumped to the wrong conclusion and she didn't correct you, I thought it was better if you believed I was in love with someone else.''

''Why?'' he demanded, looking somewhat savage in the process.

''So you wouldn't think I was after you.''

''And were you?''

She stared straight at him. Rafael had caught her with her own golden lasso. It was tight around her neck. Truth time was here at last. ''Yes.''

''Thank God!'' he cried. ''Don't you know I've been in pain ever since?'' His voice throbbed with raw emotion she could feel.

''I've been in pain too, Rafael. Your sister spoke so often of your deep love for Isabell, I couldn't imagine your ever caring for me the same way,'' came her tremulous response.

''I *don't* care for you the same way,'' he said bluntly. ''You're two different women from two different times and worlds. I was re-born that day on the beach when you saved Apolonia. You became my obsession.

"When Lianor told me you'd gone back to California, I swear I felt every bit of life drain out of me."

Her eyes fused with his. "When my secretary put the receptionist on the phone and she told me you and Apolonia were out in the foyer of Lady Windemere's, I felt every bit of life flow *back* into me.

"I love you so much, Rafael. I would have done *anything,* agreed to *anything,* to belong to you! If the puppy hadn't started howling—"

"Don't remind me."

He reached for her, crushing her in his powerful arms. They rocked back and forth, one throbbing entity of desire. "Thank God you love me and won't ever leave me. I never had any intention of finding someone else to replace Maria, not after you came into my life."

She buried her face in his neck. "I planned to become so indispensable to you, you'd want me and only me, *forever.* I adore you, darling. Love me tonight."

His groan of pleasure reverberated in her heart. "Have no fear of that. I'm going to make love to you day and night for the rest of our lives right here in our new home.''

Mallory tipped her head back to look in his eyes. ''What do you mean 'new home'?''

''The Alfama suite— This is where we're going to live from here on out.''

''I don't understand. You need it to help finan—''

''I only need it for one reason. To keep my chefs happy,'' he interrupted before plundering her mouth with his own. She grew so light-headed he picked her up and carried her to the king's bedroom.

After following her down on top of the enormous bed he said, ''Word has reached my ears that among your various activities which have taken the palacio by storm, you've been busy cooking.''

''I want to do everything for you!'' she cried.

He flashed her that seductive smile she could never get enough of. ''Since this suite has a kitchen, I've decided my wife needs her own place to perform her culinary skills for her lord and master.''

"That's what you are to me," she cried. "Till the end of time."

All mirth left his eyes. "I love you, Mallory. You've transformed my life and Apolonia's. Already you've turned us into a family. I haven't known what it was like to sit around a table with my loved one and enjoy a home-cooked meal since before my parents died. We can have it all right here, for the rest of our lives."

"Oh, Rafael—"

She felt so euphoric, she covered his face and hair with kisses. "I'm crazy in love with you, *amado*. One day I'm going to be able to say all the things I want to say to you in your own language. It's more beautiful than English. I'm so happy I want to shout it to the world."

"Shout all you want, *amada*. These walls are so thick, no one will ever hear you but me. Which is perfect because I'm the only one who needs to hear them. Over and over and over again."

Their mouths met and clung in a frenzy of longing.

278 RAFAEL'S CONVENIENT PROPOSAL

"But before I lose complete control, we have one more important thing to discuss."

She stared into those black orbs that held her heart. They blazed with desire for her, causing her to tremble. "What's that?"

"Do you want babies?"

"I want your babies more than you'll ever know. The timing is up to you."

His expression sobered. She could read his mind.

"Don't be afraid for us, Rafael. I'm strong and healthy. My mother sailed through her pregnancy. The only reason they didn't have more children was because they were older parents. I always wanted them to give me a brother or sister."

She nibbled on his lower lip. "Apolonia has already confided that she'd love one of both."

He cupped her face in his hands. "If anything happened to you—" his voice shook.

She closed her hands over his wrists. "Nothing will, darling. I feel we were fated to meet for a reason. Don't you?"

"Yes," he whispered against her lips.

Slowly they began to love each other. Unlike the other night, they took their time relishing each new discovery until the flame burned hotter, consuming them both.

"Rafael—did you hear that?"

"Hear what?" he muttered, still asleep though he held her pinioned against him. After a night of passion beyond anything she could have imagined, he'd finally fallen off.

"Someone's knocking at the outer doors."

"Ignore it. We have more pressing things to do." He pulled her head down and drank from her mouth, seemingly insatiable and ready to make love to her all over again.

"But we can't," she cried, feeling herself succumb to the passion he engendered with one caress. "I think it's Apolonia."

"Ines is looking after her."

"Darling—it's eleven o'clock in the morning."

"I don't care what time it is. I'm on my honeymoon."

The knocking grew louder. Enough that Rafael lifted himself up on one elbow.

"No else would be that persistent except your daughter," she whispered. "I'd go, but I don't even have a robe to put on."

His white smile captivated her. "No. You don't. As far as I'm concerned, you'll never wear anything when we're alone."

Heat spread over her entire body.

"You're so lovely, *amada,* I'm at a continual loss for words." He kissed her passionately on the mouth. "Keep the bed warm for me while I go see what she wants."

Rafael slid out from the covers and put on his chinos. It took him a minute to open both sets of doors.

His daughter looked up at him bright-eyed. *"Bom dia,* Papa. I decided to come and visit you. Did everything work out?" she asked in a hushed voice.

A smile broke out on his face. There had to be a better word for joy, happiness. But he couldn't think of one.

"Why don't you come in and see for yourself?"

She ran through the suite to their bedroom.

Mallory held out her arms. "Come on up here, darling. How's Flash this morning?"

"He's so sweet. I put him in bed with me for a little while. He snuggled under the covers against my leg and went to sleep until I got up."

"Sounds like everyone's happy," Rafael said, smiling pointedly at his blushing bride after joining them on top of the bed. She robbed him of breath.

"You're my real mama now, huh?"

"Yes. And you're my real daughter now." They hugged.

"Are we going to have a baby someday like Violente's parents?"

Mallory went a darker red.

"Yes," Rafael blurted. "Just as soon as possible. Which means we have to move."

Apolonia blinked. "Where?"

This was getting fun. So much fun Rafael felt euphoric. He played with the toes peeking out of his daughter's sandals. The nails were polished in a frosty pink. More of Mallory's magic handiwork.

"We thought we'd make the Alfama suite our home. I like the idea of us all learning how to cook."

"We're going to live in here in the King's apartment?" She sounded shocked at the prospect.

"Yes, *querida*. Do you like the idea?"

"I *always* wanted to live in here."

Mallory smiled at him, sending his heart skidding out of control.

"I didn't know that. Which room shall we turn into your bedroom?"

He could hear her mind racing with possibilities. She scrambled off the end of the bed and hurried through the huge apartment. While she was gone, he took advantage of the time to thoroughly kiss his wife.

He was still devouring her when Apolonia came running back.

"Can I have the music room?"

"I think that's a good choice, *querida*. It's spacious and sunny."

"We could move the piano into the sitting room," Mallory theorized. "The other bedroom could be turned into a nursery. The puppy will have two balconies to call his own.''

''That will be perfect!'' Apolonia started for the main doors. ''I've got to call Violente and tell her!''

''Don't say anything about us having a baby yet,'' he cautioned.

''How come?''

Mallory burst into laughter. It was so infectious, Rafael joined her.

''Because these things take time,'' he reminded her.

''Then hurry, Papa!'' With that heartfelt plea, she rushed out of the room.

''Yes, Papa. Hurry!'' Mallory begged. ''My parents are dying to be grandparents.''

''I forgot!'' Apolonia was back. ''Tia Lianor called early this morning. She wanted to talk to you, but I told her you couldn't be disturbed.

''She got real upset, so I had to tell her you were sleeping in the Alfama suite with mama because you loved her more than life itself.''

Mallory's blue eyes swerved to his. They were moist and eloquent with love.

"What did Lianor say to that?"

"She started crying because she was so happy. Then she hung up. I've got to talk to Violente, but I'll be back later with Flash. I want to show him his new home." She dashed away.

Rafael's throat swelled. "Our new home." He took off his chinos and got back under the covers with her. "I love the sound of that."

"So do I, darling." She kissed him hard and long. "Now about Lianor—"

"Yes?" Mallory was like a drug in his system. He couldn't get enough of her and was in no more mood for talk.

"I thought I'd ask her to drive Apolonia and me to our next tennis lesson on Tuesday."

"Tennis?"

"Yes. I heard you used to be pretty good, so I thought we ought to learn. Our instructor is gorgeous."

Ines hadn't told him about that. He stopped kissing her long enough to look at her. "How gorgeous?"

His wife's blue eyes shimmered mysteriously. "Lianor will have a heart attack when she sees him. He's single, and a former pro tennis champion from the Braga region who was injured in a car accident. It forced him to rethink his career plans.

"Now he's the head of his own computer company in Atalaia and coaches kids on the side. You'd like h—"

"You've convinced me," he said, kissing her mouth because he had to taste it again or go mad. "Right now I need convincing that last night wasn't a dream, that my generous, giving bride isn't a figment of my imagination. Love me, *amada*. Love me as if there's no to-morrow."

"Yes, Sire."

Laughter rumbled out of him before she pro-ceeded to make him feel more immortal than any man who ever lived, surely more than King Pedro himself.

MILLS & BOON® PUBLISH EIGHT LARGE PRINT TITLES A MONTH. THESE ARE THE EIGHT TITLES FOR JULY 2004

❦

THE BANKER'S CONVENIENT WIFE
Lynne Graham

THE RODRIGUES PREGNANCY
Anne Mather

THE DESERT PRINCE'S MISTRESS
Sharon Kendrick

THE UNWILLING MISTRESS
Carole Mortimer

HER BOSS'S MARRIAGE AGENDA
Jessica Steele

RAFAEL'S CONVENIENT PROPOSAL
Rebecca Winters

A FAMILY OF HIS OWN
Liz Fielding

THE TYCOON'S DATING DEAL
Nicola Marsh

MILLS & BOON®

Live the emotion

0604 Rom LP

MILLS & BOON® PUBLISH EIGHT LARGE PRINT TITLES A MONTH. THESE ARE THE EIGHT TITLES FOR AUGUST 2004

_____ ❧ _____

THE MISTRESS PURCHASE
Penny Jordan

THE OUTBACK MARRIAGE RANSOM
Emma Darcy

A SPANISH MARRIAGE
Diana Hamilton

HIS VIRGIN SECRETARY
Cathy Williams

THE DUKE'S PROPOSAL
Sophie Weston

PRINCESS IN THE OUTBACK
Barbara Hannay

MARRIAGE IN NAME ONLY
Barbara McMahon

A PROFESSIONAL ENGAGEMENT
Darcy Maguire

MILLS & BOON®

Live the emotion

0704 Rom LP